# And so it is...

*A search for equanimity and understanding*

Stephen Waters-Adams


ISBN-13: 979-8-8761-0905-7

*For June, in love and deepest gratitude*

# Preface

Although ostensibly a work of fiction, and the narrative is, indeed, a mélange of both real and imagined events, this writing is in fact no more than thinly-veiled autobiography. Perhaps that makes it little different from all fiction, for no author has anything other than his or her experience to draw on: even the most extreme flights of fantasy derive from the fears, longings and desires that we all create for ourselves as we live. But this work does not try very hard to deceive the reader and those that know me will certainly recognise facets of my nature and elements of my history throughout these pages. All names in the account are fictionalised, but of course some members of the very limited cast are drawn strongly from real people. Again, there is no other source for a writer. The over-riding motivation for its creation was to chronicle, and attempt to understand, what was happening to June, my wife of over forty years, as dementia slowly altered what the outside world could perceive of her conscious inner life. I had no idea where it would lead. I am sure that my processing of this so heart-breaking degradation of a person is not yet finished, but it has already drawn me into an unfolding awareness of existence that has cast light for me on those so human questions of life and purpose that our wonderful capacity for consciousness has thrown into the mix of our lives. It is a marvellous facility to possess, but there is, indeed, no such thing as a free lunch.

The writing is, in its introspection, thoughtful, angry, exasperated, bitter and regularly confused, but, hopefully, there is also a little lucidity thrown in, though that is frequently in short supply. It is most definitely work in progress, but there comes a point when it feels right to stand back and survey where I've got to with my exploration. On reflection, it is likely that I will in future take issue with elements of what I've written; as I say, my understanding of dementia and the mystery of consciousness is continually changing. Writing is a process, a foray into the extraordinary ability we possess to generate understanding out of the experience of the moment, and it is there that I find some kind of equanimity and solace. There is, therefore, a mix of narrative and stream of consciousness reflection in the account and I make no apology for it. Understanding is never fixed, but it is frequently portrayed as though it is, with the myriad competing perspectives which have contributed to it conveniently ignored. This writing does not have that kind of resolution. It is an evolution, generating itself from memory, history and imagination, and the competing perspectives reflect how messy, tentative and inconclusive my thinking really is. The process will not cease until I do myself. Above all, I have tried to be honest and, though the teaching passages are somewhat contrived in order to serve a greater purpose, I hope I have avoided too much self-indulgence over and above the huge self-indulgence of the project itself. I have written this for myself and in tribute and love for June, but I hope that as you, the reader, are already engaging with my tangled thoughts, you might find some interest in its pages.

Cumbria 2024

For most of his adult life, he had harboured a desire to live on the west coast of Scotland. Born and bred in the city, as he grew through his teenage years he yearned to get away, to see more of the country and to experience a life he had largely only read about. Until his father bought a car when he was fourteen, his experience of countryside had mostly been limited to an occasional cycle ride with friends into the local green belt or fishing trips to the deeply vegetated banks of a local river. Later teens had extended these excursions a little, riding pillion on his friend's scooter, but always he had to return to the stifling environment of suburbia. He dreamed of how his future life would be different.

His father had owned a copy of Johnston's Three Miles to One Inch Road Atlas of Great Britain with its fascinating contour maps coloured to represent different heights. He had spent hours poring over them, drawn to where the colours became increasingly darker brown as he followed narrow roads into the heart of upland Britain, with places attaining a quasi-mystical place in his imagination through their remoteness from his everyday experience. He had been filled with wonder as he had traced insignificant roads through the darkening ochres of the surrounding hills to find isolated houses marked only by tiny black squares. They lay in what seemed to him to be total isolation. What must it be like to live in them? The wild uninhabited heart of Wales around Pumlumon was an immediate draw to his rapt exploration, given its relative closeness to the crowded lowland England where he lived. On the maps of his home town there was confusion and turmoil; the roads were difficult to follow, the pages filled with line upon line of red or orange fighting through the jumble, with dense shading indicating the sprawling conurbations around them. They exuded the cacophony of the city and he recoiled from them. But on the maps of the hills, where the roads were so narrow they warrantied no colour to demarcate them against the browns of the hills, he could feel the freedom, as if the fresh mountain air were blowing on him from the page.

When he was eighteen, his parents decided that they, too, wanted to visit these places. It coincided with his first year at university and, on return from his first term, he was greeted with the very pleasant news that they were thinking of a holiday in Wales that summer. Before they went, they bought walking boots, a couple of cheap rucksacks and some waterproofs. There was also a trip to the local bookshop to buy some more detailed maps. These led to many more hours of study, this time planning routes into the hills, deciding with his father which they were going to climb and what would be the best routes up. He was enthralled and, during the following two terms, the excitement was never far away. When, finally, his father started up the ageing Vauxhall and they set out over the Chiswick flyover and out onto the west-bound artery of the A4, he felt as though he was being liberated from a long imprisonment, such was the sense of elation at what was to come. He had never felt so alive.

Wales had not disappointed. The cottage his parents had rented was far enough along one of those insignificant roads to feel isolated, with marvellous views of bare hillsides sweeping down to a valley bottom where a stream tumbled over its rocky bed. He felt in heaven. They spent many days on the hills, hiking over Pumlumon itself one day and even had a trip to south Wales, where they had walked up to Lyn y Fan Fach, lying under the impressive terraced cliffs of the Black Mountain. It was his first experience of true mountain architecture and he vowed it would not be his last.

After another trip to Wales the following year, they made their first visit to Scotland. If the major passion of his life had not been set firm by Wales, it would be by a visit to the Highlands. The Highlands... It was a name that had fascinated him as a child as he looked at his father's maps. He had been entranced at the way they became increasingly brown with hills as he went further North through the atlas, flicking from page to page, following the line of a road or tracing a river back to its source in the high ground. Up through the northern Pennines, past the intriguing hills of the Lake District (strangely, they had always escaped his exploration) and over the border into Scotland where, as he pushed on past Glasgow and Edinburgh, a magical land of mountains, islands and sea lay stretching out to the North and West. The maps were crowded with peaks of darker and darker brown until some achieved the rare distinction of being white, to signify great height. Strange Gaelic names that he could not pronounce filled the page, such as Ben Cruachan, Braeriach, Liathach, An Teallach or Suilven on the mainland and, even more entrancing, the remote tops of the Inner Hebrides, high above the island-studded sea: Beinn an Òir in the Paps of Jura, Ben More on Mull, and the jumble of names on the narrow ridge of the Cuillin on Skye, topped by Sgurr Alasdair. They had stirred his imagination. As he had explored the vast, uninhabited reaches of Sutherland and Caithness, to his great surprise he came across names of mountains he was familiar with. In the far, far north, the highest land included two peaks whose names had achieved national fame, through the unlikely agency of horse racing. The highest of the two was Foinaven, also the name of the extraordinary winner of the 1967 Grand National, and alongside it lay Arkle, lesser in stature as a mountain, but a truly great race horse, winning the Cheltenham Gold Cup three times in a row. He had been amazed, and it had begun a profound fascination with the northern and western Highlands and the Gaelic language that had lasted his lifetime.

Needless to say, that first trip to the Highlands had been a great success. They had stayed near the shores of Loch Broom in the north-west and he had been overwhelmed by the rugged beauty of the landscape, from the sea lochs and the myriad islands around the coast to the lochan-studded foothills of the wild, rocky hills. Water lilies bloomed in the clear fresh water of the lochans and they had once been lucky enough to see an eagle circling over the precipitous cliffs of a remote corrie. Settlements were small and the population low. He knew he had found his home.

But making it his home was a different matter. For a start, he had to work and there were very few jobs there. Then came all the trappings of life. His parents lived in the South and as they were advancing in years, he didn't wish to be so far away from them, even though they also loved the Highlands and would visit when they could. He graduated with a Zoology degree and, after a little drifting, trained as a primary teacher, taking a job where he could get one. That happened to be at a school in the centre of Worcester, about as far from the sea and the hills as he could get. But he enjoyed the job, finding a particular satisfaction in the openness of young children before the rigours and re-wiring of puberty set in. He stuck at it for ten years, with internal promotion up the scale, until he took a sideways move. He had been fortunate to be involved on some interesting in-service development and even had a secondment to start a Master's degree, a luxury from the Education Authority that would soon be ended. This would change the course of his working life. Whilst on one of the courses he had met Marie, a wonderful girl with whom he had felt an immediate affinity and it was not long before the full responsibilities of house, mortgage and then children, had determined that any move North would not be for some time.

He had, of course, returned to the Highlands for holidays. Marie shared his love of wild scenery and they had enjoyed trips there during the first years of their marriage, albeit with reduced opportunities for hiking and climbing. Marie had a disability. She was born with a genetic condition which meant that the muscles of her lower arms and legs would be affected by a neuropathy that interfered with the quality of the nerve impulse reaching them. During infancy, she had begun to display signs of difficulty with mobility and by the time she was five she had been diagnosed with peroneal muscular atrophy, otherwise known as Charcot-Marie-Tooth condition, abbreviated and known as CMT, after the people who had isolated it. The result of this condition was that the muscles would never develop properly and would slowly waste over the course of her life. It did not stop her learning to walk and leading an independent, active life, but she would never be able to run and, as she aged, she would find mobility increasingly difficult. But in her early twenties when they first visited the Highlands together, she still had the energy to walk independently and they had enormous fun tackling some low-level paths and immersing themselves in the old culture of the Gaelic heartlands. Indeed, when staying near Loch Ewe one year, she had tackled the mile hike over a rough path to see the falls on the Inverianvie river. It had rained and path was frequently treacherous underfoot, but she had battled on and was rewarded by the sight of the falls in spate. She had probably been motivated by a desire to give Brigg some time in the hills but, although tired and hurting by the time they got back to the car, she had been exhilarated by the experience. It was the most demanding walk she ever undertook. With time, priorities changed and when children arrived they needed a different kind of holiday. The visits to Scotland dwindled away. On his fortieth birthday, it had come as a shock to him to realise that it had been ten years since he had been to the Highlands. He had felt a stab of longing. When he did return, it was as if he had never been away. He didn't leave it that long again.

Retirement had not been from school teaching, but from a university position at an Education faculty. His Master's degree had led to enrolment on a PhD and this had been a passport to university work with initial and serving teachers. He had loved the job. Freed from what he had felt were many of the petty restrictions of school teaching (although, of course, universities had many of their own), he relished the intellectual freedom and stimulation that life in a university provided. Besides the enjoyment of working with more mature students, the PhD had led to research and, for a while, this had galvanised his creative and philosophical impulses. The work was demanding, but it never produced the feelings of intense tiredness he had frequently experienced in the classroom. He took retirement in his early sixties, ready for a new phase of life, but also because he could sense the future storm clouds building.

Retirement, however, had been his chance – their chance. The way was open for them to live wherever they wanted. One of their children was living abroad, in Rome, and the other was at present in London and he was well aware that his parents would not want to live anywhere near the capital. It was a young person's environment. Both children knew their parents would choose only one place to live – near the coast of the western Highlands.

The coast was the obvious place. Although there are many, many roads in the Highlands of the faint insignificant kind he had found so entrancing as a child, anything more than a cursory acquaintance with the area would be enough to convince that the romantic appeal of rugged isolation in a remote glen would not compensate for the far better weather to be had near the coast. The prevailing westerlies sent their clouds racing over the coastal strip before they loosed the majority of their rain onto the mountains. Life in a deep glen could be a very soggy affair indeed. When the rain cleared, the coast offered marvellous views of the Inner Hebrides and long, sun-filled evenings in the high summer months. Even more importantly, they needed to make sure they were near to a reasonable town, a hospital and access to carers. There also had to be good road links to the specialist facilities of the central belt. They would not be moving again and whatever they chose had to be future-proofed.

They had decided to live near Oban. In reality, there was little alternative. In the Highlands, there were better facilities in Inverness, but they wanted to be by the west coast and had they settled further north it would have meant going over to the wilder country of Wester Ross where facilities were sparse. They might have to forego the lily-studded lochans of the far north west, but Oban had many other delights for the eye, including the most wonderful outlook from the north end of town across the Firth of Lorn to the Isle of Mull. It also had a good, small hospital with an impressive range of services and with the option of transfer to Glasgow in emergency.

There is much luck involved in house buying and they had been incredibly fortunate to find a small cottage a few miles away near Achnacairn, across the Connel bridge and overlooking Lower Loch Etive. It was a traditional Highland dwelling, stone built and whitewashed, on the edge of a small settlement, yet far enough away from the nearest houses to provide the sense of space and freedom that had formed the driving motivation of their plan for so many years. Moreover, to add to the delight of its cheerful appearance, with its pretty little rocky but flower-strewn garden at the front, there was a view of Ben Cruachan from the sitting room window. Besides having a majestic profile and dominating the skyline for miles around, Ben Cruachan also held a special place in their family, for it was the first major peak he had climbed with their children. Marie had spent the day in Oban whilst they were on the mountain, seeing the sights and doing some shopping. Brigg remembered vividly the long arduous climb from Loch Awe, up past the reservoir where the path followed the water's edge for half a mile to provide the only respite during the ascent, the determination of the children, only ten and twelve, the blisters and the aching legs. But the children did not give up, even when it came to the last three hundred metres of climb where the slope became increasingly steep. It had been a hot, sunny day and by the time they made the final scramble to the summit, the children were exhausted, but elated. And what a summit: the views were stunning.

Whichever way they looked, there were rugged peaks and deep glens, with the splendid sight of Loch Etive piercing the heart of the southern Highlands, leading the eye towards Glen Coe and Rannoch Moor. To the west, the afternoon sun glinted on the Firth, bounded by Mull and the peak of Ben More, with the view opening out to the south west past Jura to the vastness of the Atlantic Ocean. They had spent a long time gazing and resting, before starting the long descent back to the car park, where Marie would be waiting to take them back to where they were camping.

He reached for the glass of Bunnahabhain on the side table by his chair. He gazed out of the window as the cool warmth spread down into his stomach. Wisps of evening cloud were forming around the summit of Cruachan. He sighed, letting the tiredness that built up each day finally take hold. Despite the beauty of the long May evening, he would go to bed soon; Marie was already asleep. He would have no trouble sleeping, even though it would not be truly dark until late and the blackbirds would be singing again by three. They had been so lucky to find the house; all in all, they couldn't have found a more perfect spot. There was so much to see, so much beauty to explore. Life was going to be so different. The door of the sitting room was open and he could hear Marie's gentle snoring across the hallway in what would normally have been the dining room. She sounded peaceful.

The first indication that something might be amiss had appeared nearly ten years before, although it was so slight that he had not noticed anything was wrong. Marie commented that she sometimes became aware that she might have to search for certain words when she was speaking; common words that are normally routine. It wasn't of great concern to either of them at first; she still read avidly and neither he nor any of their friends had noticed any difference in her speech. But fluent adult language is normally an automatic process; conversation proceeds instinctively. In a marvel of complex processing, words flow, the brain effortlessly initiating or responding with what it wants to communicate. Any interruption to the smooth progression, any demand upon other more immediate conscious processes, will always be felt first by the speaker, who will notice a heightening of subjective awareness as he or she has to intervene in the normal stream of speech to maintain fluency. If there is a moment's internal hesitation searching for the right word, the subject will notice it first. But just because it is noticed doesn't mean anything is wrong; we all experience that hesitation sometimes. We all know that feeling when a word is on the tip of our tongue and we can't quite express what we want to say; it is a normal feature of our lives. In addition, Marie was well into her fifties when she started noticing what was happening and banter between friends and colleagues had begun to be sprinkled with light-hearted comments about 'senior moments' and the inevitability of ageing. This milieu made it more likely that any slight additional problems had to become a more pronounced conscious feature before it was obvious that things weren't quite what they should be. That was what had happened for Marie.

Once she had become certain, Marie had fretted about her symptoms for a while before they decided between themselves that she ought to talk to her GP. By that time, her discomfort with what she felt as a constant struggle to maintain fluency in her speech had led her to worry that she might be developing a brain tumour. Fortunately, her doctor, a cheerful friendly and empathetic woman, had taken her seriously. Because of her neuropathy, Marie was already seeing a consultant at the Worcester Royal and her doctor agreed to contact him regarding Marie's new symptoms, asking if her next appointment could be brought forward. Marie had been relieved that her GP had acted so promptly. It was exactly what you wanted from your doctor: a recognition of their limitations and the gumption to listen to what patients were saying. If she had realised that the doctor's actions were probably influenced just as much by the fact that the GP trust was under financial incentive to show they were monitoring patients for any signs of the onset of dementia, she might not have been quite so impressed. But at least it had worked in her favour; now she just had to wait for the appointment.

That came through more quickly than she had anticipated and a little over three months later they found themselves sitting with her consultant in his bare, windowless room somewhere in the depths of the hospital. Dr. Thurleigh was a man in his fifties, greying and somewhat portly. He greeted them in his usual way; perfunctorily and with seemingly little engagement in his eyes. After indicating to them to sit, he regained his chair behind a large desk and peered at Marie's notes.

"So, what's the problem? Your doctor says something about you having headaches." he asked, without looking up.

Marie was not fazed by his manner; she was used to it by now. "I've having difficulty in finding words sometimes – common words that should be automatic. And just recently, my husband has noticed that some of my words seem to be a bit glarbled on occasion."

This was true. There had been times recently when Brigg had noticed that Marie had sometimes seemed to be substituting letters in words or missing out a word in a short sentence; not enough for her speech to be unintelligible or even discernible to a casual listener, but starting to be enough for someone to notice if they had reason to focus on the mechanics of her speech. She seemed to have been unaware that it was happening.

Dr. Thurleigh looked up, showing a flicker of interest for the first time. "In what way?"

Marie glanced at her husband. "You're the one who notices, John."

Brigg gave her a brief smile. "Yes," he said, looking back at the consultant. "Just the odd word, now and then, and hard for anyone else to pick up, I'd say." He turned to Marie again. "But they're obvious to me because I know you so well."

Dr. Thurleigh peered at him. "Examples?" he asked, his voice flat.

Brigg quelled his usual annoyance with the man's attitude; they had enough experience of him by now to know he was well-meaning. Just lacking in the bedside manner department. "It tends to be substituting or missing out the odd consonant here and there, so 'kitchen' might become 'kikken or" he added looking back at Marie again, "like you did just now."

Marie looked surprised and was about to reply, when Dr. Thurleigh, nodding as if in agreement, said: "Anything else?"

Brigg could see the concern in Marie's eyes. "I've noticed also that there are times when you might miss out a word in a sentence, like you did a moment ago. Not often, but just now and then, or use the wrong participle, so 'I'm going to the bathroom' might become 'I'm go to the bathroom'.

Marie looked a bit shocked. "You haven't told me that before."

"No, I know, I've only noticed it very recently – and it's very infrequent."

The consultant pursed his lips. He peered at Marie. "And you think you might have a brain tumour." It came out as a statement rather than a question. "Why is that?"

Marie seemed defensive and uncertain. She averted her eyes. "Well, I've having headaches as well and I've...I've," she said hesitantly, flushing slightly, "I've been worried. I couldn't think of what else could be happening." She raised her head again, regaining a little of her normal composure. "I wasn't trying to diagnose myself, I just asked Dr. Oakley if it could be a possibility."

Dr. Thurleigh raised his eyebrows. "What did she say?"

"Well, she didn't really say anything, just that she thought it would be best if I talked to you."

"So she didn't offer any kind of diagnosis?"

"No."

"And the headaches? Are they frequent?"

"Well, yes...sometimes."

"Yes, but you have always been prone to headaches," Brigg interjected. "You've had the odd migraine now and then ever since I've known you. Maybe you're more sensitive to them now because you're worried."

Marie frowned at him.

"Sorry," he said, sensing that he was being presumptuous. "That was inappropriate of me. They're your headaches, not mine."

Dr. Thurleigh was scribbling notes on a pad. When he had finished, he read through all Marie's notes again, nodding slowly. "Are you finding it is interfering with your job as a teacher?"

Brigg could see that this was a difficult question for Marie. Her job as an English teacher was very important to her. He saw her stiffen slightly. When she spoke, her voice sounded guarded. "Not with the pupils, but I'm coming more conscious of my own speech and it makes me feel awkward."

Dr. Thurleigh stared at her quizzically for a few moments. "Okay," he said quietly.

He didn't say anything for perhaps ten seconds, then seemed fixed on a decision. "I think I'd like a bit more information about your symptoms, so I'm going to ask you to see a consultant psychologist I know before we go any further. He's very experienced and he'll be able to carry out cognitive tests to analyse what seems to be going on with your speech. I don't doubt that you're feeling concerned, but I'd like his professional perspective before we go any further. He'll have a range of analytic tools at his disposal that I don't and it will help me make a decision. Is that okay?"

Marie seemed a little taken aback. She had known there could be consequences from this appointment, but this felt like a serious escalation. There was trepidation in her voice as she replied. "Oh, well, yes – I suppose so. How long will that take to come through?"

Dr. Thurleigh shrugged. "I'm not sure, but I can ask for it as quickly as possible. Maybe a month or so?"

Marie pursed her lips. "Okay," she said slowly. Brigg watched her fighting her emotions; he knew it was difficult for her. There is always a child-like hope that a doctor will be able to soothe one's concerns with reassuring words; that was not happening. He wanted to ask the doctor on her behalf whether he had any ideas about diagnosis, but knew he had to leave it to Marie. It was a frustrating outcome.

Marie saw Brigg looking at her. She stared into his eyes and shook her head very slightly, confirming that she didn't want him to intervene. She turned back to the consultant. "So, we'll come here afterwards, then? We won't have to wait for the appointment I've got booked with you, will we? That's not for nearly six months."

Dr. Thurleigh nodded. "I hope not. I can't promise it, but I'll try to make that appointment at the same time I ask for one with Dr. Peters. I will try to get it booked as a priority" He stood up; the appointment was obviously over. "You will hear very shortly, Mrs. Brigg"

In the car going home, Brigg had asked Marie why she hadn't pressed Thurleigh any further about diagnosis, but she had clammed up. Reflecting on it later that evening, he realised how traumatic the consultation had been for her. Bringing her symptoms out into the open had laid bare the fact that something potentially serious might be happening and, for the first time, she had felt frightened about the future. At that moment in the consulting room, she hadn't wanted any more challenge; she had to process this new situation first. For the first time for him, too, the reality set in that things were changing.

To their surprise, the appointment with the psychologist did come through quickly and, a month later, Marie sat a range of cognitive, reading and comprehension tests at a local clinic. Afterwards, Roland Peters, a genial man probably also in his fifties, asked if they could go for a coffee whilst he analysed the results. He smiled at their surprised expressions.

"I don't usually do this," he said; "normally I would make another appointment for a review. But Dr. Thurleigh asked it as a special favour. He knows you are anxious and, unusually, I do have some time before my next appointment. To be honest, it won't take me too long to go through these; I think I know already what they will indicate. Come back in an hour."

They sat in a local café a couple of hundred yards away for half an hour, feeling slightly embarrassed that they had misjudged her neurologist's manner for indifference, then waited the rest of the time back in the clinic.

Almost exactly an hour after they had left, Dr. Peters ushered them back into his consulting room. He smiled broadly at Marie. "It's just as I thought: I've only skimmed your results, but all of the tests seem to score in the normal range; in fact," he added, glancing at where he had entered marks on each one, "they are very normal; you score higher than average. Your reading and comprehension are very good and you only made one or two little mistakes on the cognitive test. I will, of course, prepare a full report, but I don't think it will tell us much more."

Marie looked puzzled. "So you saying that there's nothing wrong with me?"

The psychologist pursed his lips then smiled gently at her. "Not quite." He stared at her for a few moments then continued. "These tests indicate that you have full or almost full function with reading, comprehension and processing. But that doesn't mean that there isn't something happening. I've already noticed three times when you've mispronounced a word and I think you have a tendency to get a present participle wrong sometimes. You've also left out the odd word, like you did just now. You said 'So you saying' rather than 'So you are saying'. It's not frequent, but it's there." Brigg saw some relief in Marie's eyes: at last, she had confirmation it wasn't just in her imagination. Dr. Peters continued: "I'm sure you probably think this has been a waste of time, but it hasn't." He looked straight at Marie. "You feel it and I can see it; believe me, we are taking you seriously. My tests may have helped to focus our attention on the areas of the brain that we might want to explore. I will send my findings back to Dr. Thurleigh and suggest that you have an MRI. I'm sure that will be his next recommendation, anyway."

Marie looked worried. Brigg knew that the thought of an MRI was daunting; she had a tendency to feel very claustrophobic in confined spaces and had always expressed an intense fear of the idea of being inserted into the MRI tube.

Roland Peters noticed her disquiet. "I know they are rather intimidating, but you can ask for a blindfold and you can take a favourite CD with you if you like. It's all over quickly and it really would give some important information to help with the diagnosis of what's going on."

Marie was quiet, but she gave a brief smile of acquiescence.

Roland Peter's smile was broad. "It's been a pleasure meeting you, Mrs. Brigg, and you too, Mr. Brigg. I don't think Dr. Thurleigh will send you back to me, but I would see you as quickly as I could if he did." He stood up and held out his hand. "I wish you the very best for the future."

His disarming manner defused Brigg's urge to ask him to speculate about diagnosis.

He had finished the whisky. He decided against pouring another; these days he usually limited himself to one. Normally, Marie didn't need him through the night and, once the carers had left, most evenings she would settle down and sleep right through until morning. But morning was early and Brigg would be up at six – every day. He needed good, refreshing sleep and he needed to be clear headed when he woke up. He looked across to Cruachan. A front was coming in from the west and the top was now completely under cloud. But the cover was not yet complete and a shaft of sunlight illuminated the lower slopes, glinting on the rocky hillside and turning the grass golden. A sudden, unexpected wave of emotion washed over him: a mixture of sadness and longing for what might have been and a desperate pity for what was happening to Marie. All this beauty, and all this sorrow. It was not going to be like this: they were going to walk by the hills, laugh by the loch in the long summer evenings and relax in each other's love in the home they had dreamed about for so long. He wiped his eyes. No; not for them. Life was not going to relax the challenge. Perhaps it never would.

One's life seems to make sense only in hindsight. It is there that one can imagine it has had purpose and direction; that, if one has been lucky, one has been progressing towards some kind of resolution over the years. The reality is very different. Hindsight is a fabrication; there is only now. Life will always make sense looking back, whatever decisions are taken, whatever paths are followed. It is an easy, but fallacious conclusion: experience is of itself transient and, although sometimes it feels as though that transience is stretched over a lifetime, it is not purposeful of itself. Although useful in so many ways, our fixation on goal-directed behaviour obscures this fact, constantly luring us away from the reality of the present, so that most of our lives are spent anticipating tomorrow rather than appreciating today. Perhaps the resolution of our search for a purpose to life lies in the development of understanding that there isn't, actually, a goal at all. Life doesn't need purpose and direction: it is.

It had taken a little while for Brigg to settle on education as a career. His inclination to avoid people and towns had initially drawn him to seek work in areas such as nature conservation, but at the time he graduated such posts were few and far between. After a succession of casual jobs, he applied for teacher training, motivated purely by the need to get something that paid reasonably and that might have a little more interest than what he was doing. There was, at the time, a shortage of primary teachers and he had no trouble gaining a place on a PGCE. Although sceptical that he would actually finish the programme, he enrolled, and found to his surprise that he grew into the role of teacher. It wasn't anything like as daunting as he expected and he enjoyed most of his interaction with children. Later on, he reached an even stronger level of contentment when he moved to university work, working with students who were, for the most part, bright and inquisitive. Reflecting on his experience, he began to think that the most important thing you could ask of a job, after the value of the remuneration in keeping food on the table and a roof over your head, was that it would allow you experiences that helped you be aware of yourself. Other than that, it didn't really matter what you did. If you were going to use your experience, you would. Life has to be grasped; it won't give itself without effort.

When he did look back at his life, Brigg knew he had been fortunate. Not only had he had the great fortune to meet and marry Marie, with all the joys of home and family that ensued, he had also been lucky with his job, considering that he had only gone into teaching because he knew he needed more money and prospects than his casual work provided, and that if he didn't capitalise on the qualifications he had already achieved they would soon become irrelevant on the job market. Teaching had frequently been stimulating and he had felt that he was finally doing something worthwhile. If nothing else, it was always unpredictable; even the most tedious lessons could be enlivened by unplanned interactions. He knew that in many ways he was lucky being with primary children; the nature of those interactions could be much more demanding with an older age group. He used to smile wryly when he saw the glossy newspaper recruitment adverts for secondary teachers. They were characterised by their disingenuousness, always trying to ensnare the naïve. One, for science teachers, had been an absolute classic, reaching the apogee of unattainable aspiration. It depicted a science teacher standing at the front of a class, beside a workbench complete with stereotypical flasks, funnels and Bunsen burners. At the rear of the class, a teenage boy and girl eyed each other up, sniggering behind their raised textbooks. The caption read: "Your job is to make fractional distillation more interesting than sex." Fat chance of that! Not only was fractional distillation patently not as interesting as sex, Brigg knew he didn't want to live in a world in which it was. He wondered why they bothered with such tripe; they'd probably get better teachers if they represented a bit more reality in their posters.

Brigg's university position was in the science department of the education faculty. By and large, they focused on undergraduates and postgraduates enrolled on primary programmes, along with in-service work for serving teachers. His approach to teacher education was probably not quite what readers of the more popular right-wing newspapers would have imagined it should have been. Given the size of its budget, Education is always a political football and there had been much discussion of the place of universities in the training of teachers. Alternative routes into teaching had begun to proliferate, with central government assuming more of a role, sidestepping the more usual university qualifications. Universities were beginning to be seen as subversive, undermining what the government saw as clear training targets, inculcating distracting, if not downright dangerous, left-wing ideas in students' minds. The talk was always of standards and assessment, with little discussion of the notion of education itself.

Along with many of his colleagues, Brigg had viewed these developments with increasing disquiet. He had not gone into teacher education simply to train students to jump through hoops. He believed passionately that it was right to involve universities in the process, and the increasing government control over what had to be taught contradicted that principle. Universities were about personal intellectual enquiry and the freedom to develop ideas; to attempt to regulate and standardise teacher thinking during a student's course was not only tiresome and a waste of talent, it also had sinister overtones of a move towards increased social control. Brigg was determined that, whilst teacher education programmes were still located in universities, the programmes he was involved with would retain the kinds of challenge that would enable students to analyse for themselves the goals and purposes of the profession they were entering. Of course he would cover curriculum targets (funny how the certainty of one year would give way to the revised truth of the next government edict), but he did not see that as his main aim. He wanted students to explore and understand what science was: not only its knowledge and the possible strategies for teaching it, but its process and philosophy. He wanted students to reflect upon what function science fulfils and why human beings engage in it. What sort of knowledge does it provide? How did it contribute to our understanding of the human condition? They were questions one could ask of any subject, and Brigg believed one should. Without an understanding of the purpose and philosophy of a subject in the journey of human experience, how could one adequately introduce young people to it?

Some of his most satisfying sessions were spontaneous, extemporising from his general aims for the seminar, not only challenging students' knowledge but forcing them to engage with deeper questions of experience and reality. It was when this happened that Brigg felt most alive in his teaching. It was no longer a job; it was engaging him, too, in an exquisite consciousness of his own existence. It was after these sessions that he would reflect that he had been very lucky in his career.

*The seminar room is a general purpose classroom, with tables and chairs organised in groups. Along one wall, a row of windows faces south and the sunlight is streaming in. The students who arrived early have chosen to sit at the tables close to these windows, enjoying the relaxation of the late autumn afternoon. They are chatting happily to each other, flicking through their phones. Brigg watches them. They seem oblivious to him and to the beauty of the cold blue sky; they will only notice the sun by its absence, once it has sunk below the rooftops of the flats across the road. It will not be long. The room is warm, but there is an ominous chill in the November air outside. Winter will soon be here. He feels a sharp jolt of consciousness of his own existence. He is remembering himself, as Gurdjieff liked to say. The room has become hard, his focus sharp and clear. The chatter of the students fades and he is aware only of things: hard, precise things in space. Invisible strands emanate from his perception to all points of the room, holding it all in a web of existence he has created. It is trying to say something. He leans on it, feeling the presence of the things as much as seeing them. Each one: each table, each chair, each student makes a hole in space. Everywhere there are holes in space. What fills them? It is unnerving. It is absurd: why him, here, now? Everywhere there are holes in space; holes that he fills with his imagination. The room is filling up. He watches the students a little longer. The newcomers are as oblivious to him as the others. They fill the chairs, content in their state, unaware of the turmoil gripping a mind only metres from their own. Only one is looking at him. She smiles. It breaks the spell. He sends a flicker back and the room fades. He cannot hold onto what it was saying and he feels a loss. It is not unknowing that brings dissatisfaction; it is the knowledge of our unknowing that fuels our angst. The student has turned away to her friends. Sometimes it is best to embrace oblivion.*

*But he will not. He puts his session notes to one side and takes hold of an unoccupied chair. The tables are placed around the room, leaving a space in the centre. He picks up the chair and places it there. The students have stopped talking; they are now watching him curiously. He smiles at them.*

*"Indulge me."*

*Brigg turns to the student who had brought him out of his reverie by her smile.*

*"Could you sit here for a moment, Megan?"*

*The student looks surprised, but gets up and moves to the chair. They know him well and are comfortable in his sessions. Brigg now has the full attention of the room. He waits until the student has settled herself, just a little self-consciously, then addresses the others.*

*"Where's Megan?"*

*He notices the amused frowns on their faces. A male student, smiling, gives the obvious response:*

*"Er...on the chair, John. You've just put her there."*

*"You're sure she's there?"*

*The student laughs. "Of course I am!"*

*Brigg scans the room; there is an air of puzzled amusement.*

*"So, Megan's on the chair. Is that what you all think?"*

*The students concur.*

*"How do you know?"*

*The first student responds. "Obviously, we can see her, John."*

*"Are you sure?"*

*"Yep.""*

*Brigg nods. "Mmm...okay." He addresses the room.*

*"I presume you all agree with Toby?"*

*There is a ripple of good-humoured affirmation.*

*"Tell me what you can see, then."*

*The students offer descriptions of Megan from where they are sitting – back, side, front, her face, her clothes, her posture. He acknowledges their replies, then asks how they can be so certain they are looking at Megan. One of the students from Megan's table says with a slight hint of frustration:*

*"Because I can see her, John. She's just moved there and sat down; what more do you want me to say?"*

*Brigg knows that the questioning will soon start to irritate them and wonders if he should carry on. Always he is questioning, trying to upset the acceptance his students bring to the world. Is he simply indulging himself? Maybe this isn't the right time to try to disturb their equilibrium.*

*The moment passes. To be human is to be conscious and to embrace the disquiet that accompanies what we assume to be the one feature that places us apart. It is his job to encourage that knowledge of ignorance. To educate is to draw out potential; the students have signed up for this.*

*Megan is smiling, but also looking bemused. She adjusts her position in the chair: she can sense that this may take a little longer than she thought.*

*Brigg ignores the student's frustration. He singles out a male student sitting by the window.*

*"Do you agree with the rest of them, Carl?"*

*"Of course."*

*"Ok then: what exactly can you see of Megan?"*

*The student seems pleased to be asked. He observes Megan carefully, describing hair, clothes, skin and focusing on details such as colour, shine and shape. His accuracy is impressive.*

*Brigg nods in approval. "That seems pretty comprehensive. So, you are confident that you can see Megan."*

*"Yes: she's sitting there in front of us."*

*Brigg pauses, then asks:*

*"Exactly which part of Megan do you think you can actually see?"*

*Carl notices the serious edge in Brigg's voice. He hesitates slightly before replying and frowns, trying to work out what he might have missed.*

*"All of her, from my side at least: body, clothes, hair, like I've just said..."*

*"Ok," Brigg accepts. "How did you see that?"*

*The student responds dryly:*

*"With my eyes, John – obviously."*

*The student is beginning to get annoyed and Brigg notices that he is also losing the attention of some of the others. Time to push it a little.*

*"Your eyes. How did they do that?"*

*The student stumbles; he's not too strong with physics.*

*"By...by picking up the light coming from Megan."*

*"Coming from Megan? Is it Megan's light?"*

*Hesitation. "No...but it's coming from her into my eyes."*

*A ripple of conversation spreads around the rest of the group. They are now a little more engaged again. Another student comes to the rescue.*

*"There is light in the room and it's bouncing around. Some of it bounces off Megan and some of that will bounce into our eyes. That's how we can see her."*

*"What do you mean by her?"*

*"Well, her colour; her shape."*

*Another chips in.*

*"It's different colours because Megan's clothes or her flesh absorb some of the wavelengths, meaning that only some*

*of them reach us. Depending on which type – red, green, blue, or different mixtures, we see the different colours."*

*Brigg nods at this piece of information.*

*"So, Megan absorbs some of the light and the rest comes back to you. That bit that you get: is that Megan?"*

*The student hesitates.*

*"Well, sort of..."*

*Brigg smiles. "Are you sure? Is it all of her, or just a bit?"*

*The student looks anything but sure.*

*"It's the bit facing me, I suppose..."*

*There is now a good level of engagement in the group. Brigg continues:*

*"This is very interesting. Let's think a bit more about that light reaching your eyes: would you say that it contains anything of Megan?"*

*Discussions break out around the room. Megan looks at her fellow students, smiling:*

*"I've always said there was more to me than meets the eye!"*

*"Precisely," agrees Brigg.*

*He scans the group.*

*"Well?"*

*A student called Phoebe at the back of the room hazards a suggestion:*

*"The light can't exactly contain anything of Megan, but it's coming from where she is."*

*"So, does that mean you can see her?"*

*"Well...yes, I suppose so."*

*"But you've just told me that all you are picking up is light that is bouncing around the room. How is that Megan?"*

*One of the others is getting irritated by Brigg's questions; she wants to defend common sense. She interjects, a little forcibly:*

*"This is silly, John. It's not actually Megan, but it's been changed by interaction with her body and we see the result of that interaction. If Megan weren't there the light wouldn't have changed. It tells us where she is and what she looks like."*

*Brigg nods in agreement, wanting to keep the involvement but wishing to defuse her annoyance.*

*"Fair enough; that makes sense." He smiles at her. "But, I'm afraid I still have to ask my question, Holly: can you actually see Megan?"*

*The irritation is not yet defused.*

*"Of course I can! She's there!"*

*Brigg is actually quite pleased he has provoked a reaction. He wants them to question what he is doing and why. Hopefully they know him well enough by now to understand that there is a reason he's doing this. He scans around the group, watching their interactions and feeling himself the impact of his own questions. He feels a detachment again, isolated from the otherness coming to him through his eyes, sensing the tenuousness of perception and its horrific corollary of ignorance. What is his place in this world? Everywhere there are holes in space.*

*He calms his feelings and smiles at the student.*

*"Okay, I take your point. Just bear with me for a little longer, though."*

*Holly says nothing.*

*Brigg turns away from her and looks at the rest.*

*"The light that contains information about Megan: does that just fall on your eyes?"*

*Another student joins in.*

*"No, of course not. It's falling all over our bodies. It's just that our eyes are the part that can make use of it."*

*"How do they do that, Vicky?"*

*She seems to be confident with her biological knowledge.*

*"They are able to focus it on the retina at the back of the eye, where there are special cells which can form an image of Megan...though it's actually upside down"*

*"What sort of cells?"*

*"Very specialised cells which are sensitive to light. There are two types – rods and cones - and they respond to different intensities and wavelengths, making it possible to see in very low light as well as bright."*

*She appears pleased with her explanation.*

*Brigg nods in acknowledgement.*

*"This image: would you be able to see it if you were somehow able to look in the eye at the same time?"*

*Vicky hesitates; she's never thought of it like that before.*

*"Well..."*

*Brigg tries to help her out.*

*"You've said it would be upside down. Is it sitting on the retina, like the image you'd get in a pinhole camera?"*

*Vicky is unsure.*

*"Perhaps...I don't know."*

*There is more discussion around the room. Megan gets out her mobile phone. The screen shines brightly.*

*Help comes from another student at Vicky's table.*

*"No, it's not like that; it doesn't stop there. You have to think of the light as energy. When that energy falls on the special cells, it triggers them to send a message to the brain."*

*"What do you mean, a message?" Brigg asks.*

*This student is confident.*

*"A nerve impulse; it goes down the optic nerve."*

*Brigg smiles.*

*So, what does that impulse look like? Is it a small image of Megan, travelling along the nerve?"*

*There is laughter. The student grins.*

*"Of course not. It's a kind of electrical impulse transmitted through the cells."*

*Brigg grins back.*

*"It doesn't sound much like Megan."*

*The student agrees.*

*"No, it's not, is it? But when it reaches the brain, the brain..."*

*She stops, as if suddenly aware of an implication of her explanation.*

*"What happens there?" asks Brigg.*

*"The brain...creates an image of Megan..."*

*The student is staring at him; she is frowning, as if thinking hard.*

*"An image..." repeats Brigg gently. "Where is that? Could I see your image of Megan if I looked in your brain?"*

*The student gives a thin smile at the absurdity of the proposition.*

*"No, of course not. It's an image in my consciousness, not a physical image..."*

*She looks away, unsettled. There are some heated discussions going on around the room.*

*"Ah, your consciousness," says Brigg. "So that's where we will find her..." He smiles at the student. "I wonder, Amanda, if you have the same image of Megan as I do?"*

*Amanda does not reply, looking at her friends for support. Brigg lets the students work through their own understanding. Some will take it merely as an interesting explanation, others will appreciate deeper, more disturbing, meanings. There are holes in space, everywhere. Eventually he asks, quietly:*

*"So, if we go back to my original question, where's Megan? Have we found her now?"*

*In the pause before anyone replies, Megan's mobile phone screen flickers. She looks at the images of her friends moving across it, her brain finding pattern and form in the light of varying wavelength being transmitted by the screen. She is drawn into the world inside. Brigg looks away as reality begins to crumble.*

What's in a name? A lot, sometimes. When it comes to medicine, illness and disease, we want a name. A name tells us that we are not alone, that doctors know about our condition and probably can do something to help. That's what they are for. We are conditioned to put our trust in them; they always have an answer. Except sometimes they don't and the name they come up with is no help either.

Primary Progressive Aphasia is what they called it. It sounds impressive. It's certainly long, which probably means it holds a wealth of medical knowledge within, distilled into its common abbreviation of PPA. Once one has cracked the code of medical jargon, one will have access to the decades of research behind it, giving insight into the causes of the condition and how to cure it. There will be a pill, or perhaps a course of treatment at hospital. Not, however, with this name. For all its medical impenetrability, it means nothing. It is the equivalent of going to the doctor with a pain in your knee and then being told that your condition is well known in the medical community and has the official name of 'pain in the knee' or, perhaps more accurately, 'unexplained pain in the knee.' Primary Progressive Aphasia: it has no meaning other than a purely descriptive one. Primary: it just seems to have developed from nowhere, with no known relationship to anything else about you; Progressive: it's going to get worse, as if you hadn't realised by now; Aphasia: you're having difficulty with your speech and understanding. To quote Basil Fawlty, it states the bleedin' obvious, and it gets you precisely nowhere. Oh, and all those decades of research and the development of treatments? They don't exist. The medical profession has no idea what causes it and even less idea of what to do about it. Sorry, but your brain is slowly giving up the ghost and there will be a long slide into total gaga-ness and demise. Love to help you, but we can't. However, come back in six or nine months and we'll monitor how you're doing. At least you can become a 'case'; it will be quite interesting for us, maybe even leading to a contribution to a paper sometime, and it will maintain our position as your 'consultant', even though we already know we won't be able to do anything but watch your decline. For the more gullible (or shall we say less cynical) amongst you, it will maintain that touching faith you have in the medical profession to look after you, and that will be good for your morale.

The MRI that Roland Peters had anticipated showed a slight shrinkage of her left cerebral hemisphere. Dr. Thurleigh's face was impassive as he imparted the results to Marie; he already knew that there was going to be very little else in his medical kitbag. Her brain was shrinking and it was affecting the speech and language centres. It had nothing to do with a tumour, so she could stop thinking she had brain cancer. Ha! Fancy thinking you had a condition that we knew something about and potentially could treat... It had nothing to do with her CMT, either. No, the implication of these results was that what she was experiencing now was going to get worse as those speech and language centres deteriorated and other functions were affected. Reflecting on the appointment later, Brigg was grateful that Dr. Thurleigh had been honest and that he had seemed genuinely to regret that he had nothing to offer except ideas about managing symptoms. Speech therapy would be a good place to start; it would give Marie some ideas about how to cope with what was going to be a long decline in her ability to communicate. Slightly more animated, he therefore declared that he would arrange an appointment with a speech and language therapist, seemingly relieved that he could at least offer something. After all, the idea for any doctor that you had nothing to offer a patient apart from empty words must be very hard to take. Unless one treated medicine as a purely academic pursuit, its raison d'etre was to cure and maintain health. Impotence in the face of suffering was not an option. There was always something one could so. Thurleigh talked about advances in technology and the range of software programs specifically designed to help with communication if word-finding and speech became difficult in future. Marie said very little as he talked, her gaze distant; Brigg wondered what effect the knowledge must be having. He looked on in pity, wishing he could somehow take it away from her: give it to himself; anything to take the pain away. He felt his eyes welling.

When Marie did speak, she was calm and direct, addressing the elephant in the room.

"How long?"

Dr. Thurleigh looked at her long and hard. He knew what she was asking and he knew he had to maintain honesty.

"The truth is, I don't know. You are still relatively young – only in your fifties – so you may be able to use the software and communicate for another eight or ten years, but I'm afraid that your understanding will also start to slip at the same time as your speech deteriorates."

"So, really, we are talking about dementia, aren't we?"

Dr Thurleigh breathed deeply. "A form of, yes, though I don't find the term particularly helpful; it covers such a wide range of conditions. It is classified as a type of fronto-temporal dementia. I'm sorry."

Marie nodded. She looked straight at him. "Will it kill me?"

The neurologist was too experienced to be fazed by such direct questioning and Marie was obviously an intelligent and, for now at least, articulate woman. He had to remain candid in his replies. Watching their interaction, Brigg could tell by Thurleigh's demeanour that Marie's case had also affected him. Life could be so cruel, so random and cruel.

Dr. Thurleigh held her gaze and when he spoke it was as if, for a moment, the veneer of professional distance had been removed. His voice carried a humanity that they had not heard during any of their many consultations over the years.

"That's a difficult one to answer but yes, any form of dementia is, unfortunately, a one-way ticket, as you probably realise. I can't say how exactly it will develop, or how long it might take and you never really die of dementia, as such. Sometimes it's an infection, like pneumonia, or maybe a stroke." He looked from Marie to Brigg and addressed them both, as a couple. "With some people I might be more guarded about what I am saying, but I know you will go away and research this online, anyway. I will not insult you." He pursed his lips, then added, taking the extraordinary step for him of using Marie's first name: "Given your age, Marie, you should still have many years of enjoyable active life ahead of you before you reach that position. I don't want to be patronising, but you should think about how you are going to make the most of the next years whilst you can."

A flicker of a smile played around Marie's lips. "Thank you," she said quietly.

They came away from the consultation with a list of websites for further information and the addresses of local aphasia groups for Marie if she wanted more social contact. There was also the prospect of an imminent appointment with a speech and language therapist. They made love that night, bound by a closeness that bordered on desperation, their bodies pressed tightly together as they searched to break the maddening boundaries of individuality that ultimately keep us all apart. Brigg held Marie close, aching to be absorbed into her soft flesh so that he could share the pain with her, closing his eyes in the warmth of her embrace as they moved towards the momentary oblivion of climax. But always there is separateness and though they lay entwined for some time, Marie eventually rolled away, and into her own world. Brigg lay in turmoil as she began to cry. There was no sound other than the sob of her breathing as her tears flowed. He knew it had to come out and he made no move to comfort her further as his own emotions rose. He turned on his side, anguished at the space between them. He was alone; he would always be alone. He stared out at the room. There was a chair and a dressing table near him. Suddenly, the chair sprang into prominence, its presence hard and real, followed by the dressing table and the rest of the room. As his eyes opened wide with concentration in the dim light, he was sharply aware of his position on the bed, of Marie beside him, of the furniture, and the walls of the room. Once again, just as had happened in the lecture room with the students, he felt strands stretching out from his consciousness, holding everything in a web with him at the centre. As before, he felt a meaning just beyond his imagination. But this time, his awareness was not just confined to the room. It expanded beyond the walls and he was conscious of their place in the road outside and the vastness of the sky and space above them. He had become a point, a centre, around which the universe was revolving and at that moment it was impossible to conceive of it without him. He lay rigid and open-mouthed, gripped by a terrifying dichotomy: either existence consisted of myriad lonely points of untouchable isolation or he was all there was. He battled to hold on to the state, to make sense of it, to wrest from it a secret that lay just beyond his bursting mind. It could not be like this, it could not! But it would not yield to his interrogation and he lay rigid, cold with sweat; a single point in an incalculable immensity.

He became aware of Marie stirring beside him. She put an arm over his side, searching for comfort and he turned towards her, slipping his arm under her shoulders and drawing her to him. She buried herself into the crook of his neck and draped her leg over his, slipping quickly into sleep. The sensation of her body against his was exquisite. The terror subsided, to be replaced by a glow of acceptance; he felt her more keenly than he had ever done. He immersed himself in his sense of touch, that interface between his discrete existence and the world of conscious perception in which he lived. She was there, beside him and inside him; a reality he could not explain but of which he was certain. He closed his eyes to the world, slipping into a warmth of physicality, aware of a potential within him that he had not realised before. Before long, he had joined her in sleep.

Perhaps the most poignant irony of Marie's developing condition was that she was a person who had devoted her life, both personally and professionally, to language and to words. She had always had a love of books and read avidly, devouring novel after novel at what Brigg considered to be a phenomenal rate, keeping a log of each one she read, including a brief synopsis and critique. She belonged to two book clubs, attended local book fairs and each summer travelled down to Dartington Hall in Devon with two friends for the annual literary festival, at which notable literary worthies would talk about their latest publications, and discussion of all things literature and writing would fill the sunlit lawns and medieval granite halls until late into the evening. Professionally, her career had seen her teach at a variety of schools, including a short but rewarding spell at a Pupil Referral Unit in which she strove with mixed success to motivate disaffected youngsters to grasp the basics of competence in literacy, knowing it would possibly be the single most important achievement they could take from their formal education. She always fretted over those she could not help, those who through fault of circumstance not nature were barred from their birthright as humans. She undertook postgraduate training in the teaching of dyslexia and used that in her final work, which was to give special tutoring for those with specific learning difficulties. It was fair to say that language was her passion.

Now it was gone. Now, what verbal communication that was left was reduced to inarticulate sounds: sounds often strung together in what approximated to a sentence, but sounds that were unintelligible to anyone else. Frustration developed. As Brigg asked her to repeat again and again, searching for some clue as to meaning within the impenetrable barrage, she would become first tired, then furious at his uncomprehending expression. He would search desperately for the vaguest hints of words within her utterances, sometimes catching what he thought were syllables or even parts of syllables, repeating back to her a possible interpretation, hoping against hope that he was correct. Sometimes he was and he would feel waves of relief as her frustration subsided and the dying embers of communication between them flickered into life again. But as time went on, the flame became weaker and the frustration grew. She would stare at him, repeating her garbled speech with increasing ferocity, her eyes wide with anger that he was still uncomprehending. He knew that in her increasingly confused grasp of reality, she was imagining he was doing it deliberately. Away from the agonising passion of the encounters, he realised that this was probably perfectly logical for her. Within her deteriorating brain, she was still making perfect sense and she was simply talking to him, just as she always had. Why couldn't he understand? Sometimes, the anger that filled her was so much that Brigg had to walk away, unable to cope with the pain of the assault and the spectacle of her failing mind. Few days passed without tears.

Marie was a fiercely independent woman, justifiably proud of what she had achieved in her life and career. Because of her disability, everyday life had presented so many more challenges than the average person would encounter. When she was young, the idea of disabled access to buildings or managing environments for inclusion so that physical ability did not limit participation, was almost non-existent. Stairs abounded; lifts would not work. Little was different once she was working. Meetings would be routinely booked for first floor rooms, without any thought that this might constitute a problem for some. Marie would struggle up steep flights, to arrive tired, hurting and late. Sadly, Education was no different from any other field. Once, at a training day held a little before Christmas at a local teachers' centre, she found the stairway festooned with decorations and the banister wreathed in holly. On complaining, she was told by one of the organisers, in an aggressively defensive tone, that 'nobody had told them that someone like you was coming'. Marie left. Even in later life, she and Brigg had lost count of the number of times they had visited stately homes only to be ushered into a side room where they could look at lovely photographs of all the upper and lower rooms and the kitchen. These were presented as some kind of triumph of inclusion, taken to the ultimate when there might be an accompanying video. They gave up visiting historic houses that were somehow so precious that they could not install a lift. Like many women, she had faced the question of whether to continue to work whilst raising a family and she had chosen to take an extended maternity leave whilst the children were very young. This had meant the possibility of more financial stress on both of them, but fortunately, it had coincided with Brigg's move to university work with, initially, a welcome boost to his salary. Marie loved being a full-time mum, her satisfaction tempered only by the bigotry of society against non-working women. She became part of an invisible sub-class of people to be patronised, people who suddenly found that society ignored them, adopting an unspoken attitude that they no longer had any right to an opinion – or whether they were even capable of one. Unfortunately, Marie found, she encountered this attitude in some of her female colleagues, particularly those who had chosen to place their children in child care settings and continue with work. Their condescension was frequently the strongest, as if they had to defend at all costs their own decision to remain at work. Marie never judged them, each person or couple had to make the best decisions for themselves, and she had been both hurt and disappointed that those whom she thought were friends as well as colleagues had adopted such an arrogant and unthinking attitude.

The effect of these experiences was that Marie's resilience as a person strengthened. From someone who had always had an interest in social justice and the underdog in society but who had been hampered in her agency by a natural introversion, she developed into a centred, articulate defender of the rights of women, minority ethnic groups and people with disabilities. The irritation caused by people's condescension towards her as a non-working mother became a catalyst for the growth of a determination to overcome her natural reticence and to speak up for herself and others, so that she did not let the ignorant remarks of friends and colleagues pass without comment. This led to many awkward moments, both domestically with friends and with colleagues at work, when someone busily propounding the clichés of sexist or racist views would find their statements challenged. Many could not cope with the embarrassment as Marie's incisive questioning exposed the unexamined nature of their opinions and they began to give her a wide berth. Friends dwindled, but Marie was happy with that. At one point, she had a brief spell in the Labour Party, but found she could not conform to the stifling uniformity of party politics.

Life is full of compromise and the art of achieving compromise is one of the most important prerequisites for the development of a peaceful and productive society. It rests on the ability of participants to empathise with each other and to curb tendencies towards arrogance or indifference. As Marie got older, she developed the ability to temper her own anger at those whose ignorance caused such unthinking behaviour towards minorities, and could handle people with much more tact and tolerance than they might have shown to her. However, she did not suffer fools and was intensely irritated by those who thought their opinions had a veracity that precluded all others. A reasoned life demands a search for truth, but the epistemological reality is that such truth is always impossible to find. She and Brigg had always discussed the paradoxes of life and the frustration of unanswered questions. That deep, underlying search for meaning had been what had drawn them together in the first place. Although shy, Marie was naturally more gregarious than he was; for Brigg, two people in a room was usually one person too many. Marie had been good for him and she had enabled him to open out from his solipsist tendencies and realise the value of other people's opinions.

Yet, if one's life is to count for anything, one must be true to one's reason. As a young man, Brigg sometimes found defending his ideas difficult when in company, his aversion to other people leading him to avoid confrontation. At times, he would appear to blow with the wind, bending to the loudest voice, even if he knew he disagreed. He did not think argument had any purpose and sought solitude again as soon as he could. But there is a duty to place one's own viewpoint in the wider world. Understanding evolves and it evolves most quickly and productively through interaction. That interaction does not always have to be face to face with other people, but to avoid live exploration of ideas is an opportunity missed. It is only through the dynamics of interaction – through the 'conversation' that Hans Gadamer considered so vital – that any understanding, albeit temporary and subject to change, will develop. Without the willingness of participants to the conversation to put forward their viewpoints honestly and without arrogance, such understanding will be of little value.

Marie's slow decline over the years was hard for Brigg, but he knew that it had been much, much worse for Marie herself. There is a caricature of dementia frequently portrayed in television drama, or in those nauseating snapshots of care homes that are so often used in news bulletins, where groups of old people, some with very little centred life left, are engaged in well-meaning, yet inane, activity or entertained by singing songs by George Formby or 'The White Cliffs of Dover'. They are old, so, of course, they must have been around in the thirties and the Second World War, so they must have loved those songs, even when they were very young – and we know that singing will bring back memories. Ah...bless them. Such caricatures do nothing but demean their subjects, whilst reassuring a largely uninterested public that they are being well-looked after, allowing any nagging guilt that society might not be geared up for accommodating this rather disturbing minority to be assuaged. We can forget about them, thank heavens; after all, they tend to be rather unsavoury and we've got lives to get on with. We conveniently forget that it might happen to us...

If only the transition to complete gaga-ness was immediate and consistent. If it were, dementia would not be something to be feared, for one would not know what was happening and life could carry on quite happily in a world away with the fairies. But it is not. The transition is painfully, tragically, heartbreakingly slow and it is not a steady process, however inexorable. The worst parts of the onset of dementia are not the episodes of confusion and the loss of touch with reality; those are the times when, although distressing for onlookers, the sufferer is unaware that anything is wrong. No, the worst times are the moments of lucidity, when it becomes terrifyingly apparent to the individual what is happening to them. In those moments, they can be so overwhelmed by the horror of it all and the sense of dread at their impending demise, that some will decide they can't go on. They will choose to end it all, or reach a pact with their partners or spouses to help end it for them. Such actions can only be viewed as profound expressions of compassion, no matter how problematic for society. To watch that flash of realisation transfix a loved one's expression, to see the fear in the eyes and to hear the howl of anguish it can produce, is perhaps the most terrible, gut-churning experience one can have. Brigg saw it happen with Marie, playing out over years, at first mildly, then reaching a dreadful intensity as her speech finally faded, her ability to read slipped away and her very identity began to dissolve. Those were very dark times and they imparted a real urgency into their move to the Highlands. He knew they would soon pass the point when it would be feasible, or when Marie would gain any benefit from achieving the goal she had set with him years before. In the event, they had enjoyed little more than a year exploring their new world before the cruelty of her condition reduced Marie to the confines of her home, and latterly her bed, for much of the time.

People without any experience of dementia usually have one of two reactions on meeting someone with the condition. They either feel revulsion, in which case they do their utmost to distance themselves from the sufferer, or they feel inadequacy and pity, in which case they usually adopt the approach to interaction they would normally reserve only for very young children. Both responses do little for the person with dementia, with, ironically, the latter often producing the most irritation, even though it is meant with the best intentions. As with any disability, people with dementia do not want pity. They are who they are, at that moment. We all live in the moment; there is nowhere else. Someone with a disability does not benefit from you projecting an alternative world upon them, feeling sorry that they are not someone else. They are who they are, where they are. The only way to engage is to treat them as you would anyone else: with dignity and compassion. Giving them dignity allows them the option of agency in the world, whether or not they have the mental capacity to make that agency rational; treating someone with compassion promotes a care for one's fellow human engaged on life's unfathomable quest that is equal to the care one would give to oneself, for no-one has a monopoly on the right path to take. Who is to judge whether, as the shrinking brain changes and re-wires, the insights it generates are better or worse than the 'normal'?

Marie found the increasingly pitying attitude adopted by some of her friends tiresome and it was particularly annoying when they started completing her sentences for her. In those middle days of the progression of the condition, when she would readily start a sentence in an effort to remain an active participant in conversation, she frequently had to stop, searching for words that would not come. It was a natural response to try to help her, either suggesting words for her or simply filling in what felt like an embarrassing pause by taking up the conversation again, presuming one knew where she wanted it to go. After initial displays of frustration, Marie slowly withdrew as her agency was taken away. Brigg knew that at times he had had been as guilty as others of doing this to her and he had resolved again and again to make the effort to let her engage, but with only partial success. Such was the underlying strength of the impulse. As her condition worsened and her ability even to start intelligible sentences faded, people took away all control, giving her a moment to stutter and make a few unintelligible sounds whilst they nodded in agreement at a meaning they had no idea of, then talked over her, taking up the conversation again so that it would not fall into the embarrassing, uncomfortable space where all that was apparent was a poor, confused woman rambling and stuttering in her detached reality. It was at moments like those that Brigg felt the most anguish, for he could see the exasperation in Marie's eyes that she could not express what she wanted to say, yet he also so often felt the need to keep things going, so that others would feel comfortable. He would feel wretched, about himself and about the need to carry on with social contact for her. They slowly withdrew, their friends continuing to dwindle away.

Some people with dementia retain the ability to care for themselves for a long time, but the inevitable outcome of the degradation of the brain is that, eventually, that ability eventually fades. Seven years after her diagnosis and shortly after they had finally moved to their new house near Oban, Marie started to display obvious signs of incontinence. It was only with hindsight that Brigg realised that the first inklings that something was wrong may have occurred a few years before, but neither of them, nor her GP, had realised the connection in those early days. Marie had begun to complain of regular constipation. Her GP, in her sunny, positive way, prescribed Fybogel high fibre drink, lots of water and to keep exercising as much as possible, for that would stimulate the bowel. For a time, Marie battled on, aided occasionally by an extract of senna pods. None of them linked the constipation with her Aphasia, for that was still only causing relatively mild symptoms and neither Brigg nor Marie considered the topic of constipation relevant to their once-yearly consultations with Dr. Thurleigh. However, the problem did not just lie in a lack of water in the large bowel; to put things bluntly, Marie was beginning to forget how to push. She would sit on the toilet for an increasingly long time, in obvious discomfort, sometimes straining, sometimes merely trying to mimic an action that was fading from her physical repertoire of reflexes. Her stools would become impacted and there was frequently much pain and blood from a stretched sphincter when they were eventually passed. The use of laxatives became more frequent and they were soon initiated into the sometimes alarming range of effects brought on by different kinds, from gentle stimulation to something much more explosive.

The situation was still manageable at the time they moved and, for a time, enabling Marie's bowel movements became a normal, if slightly irksome, part of their usual routines. But the change to her brain was inexorable and more symptoms would soon be felt. Shortly after arriving in the Highlands, they decided to buy a new bed; after all, their current mattress was old, over ten years, and Marie had indicated strongly that, anyway, she didn't like the style of the bed in their new bedroom. Brigg agreed and they enthusiastically went down into Oban to find one. It was fun choosing furniture; somehow, talking about such an intensely domestic subject and discussing delivery details for their new address consolidated the still unreal notion that they were now actually resident in the Highlands. They came home excited, impatient for the six-week delivery period to pass. When it finally arrived, they got excited again and both agreed that it was better-looking and more comfortable than the old one. One week later, Marie was incontinent at night for the first time.

Accidents happen, to all of us. Incontinence accidents are rare, but not unknown, so Brigg wasn't unduly concerned; he certainly didn't imagine it was to become a regular occurrence. The most irritating thing was that he had to dry and clean the new mattress. That took most of a day, with much use of a hairdryer and copious amounts of air freshener. By the evening, all was dry and he thought little of it. However, after the second time about ten days later, he ordered a waterproof mattress cover. By the fourth, it was obvious that

Marie's bladder control was deteriorating quickly. Marie, of course, was distraught. When Brigg suggested that she might begin to wear night-time incontinence pants, she was very resistant and it took all the powers of his persuasion to convince her that it would be the best thing to do. Finding them online was his introduction to the world of incontinence products, of which most people are, quite understandably, completely unaware.

The increasing incontinence seemed to be a harbinger of things to come. Now, the rate of deterioration of Marie's physical condition, as well as her mental, began to increase. For a few months, Brigg had managed all of her personal care by himself, but as each change became more of a struggle and Marie became increasingly distressed at his manhandling as he turned and lifted her on the bed in order to pull pants up or down, it became obvious to him that he would have to ask for help. The response from the health and social services was excellent. One phone call had initiated a wave of visits from doctors, community nurses, the memory team, occupational therapists and the adult social care team, all of whom offered huge amounts of advice and practical support that Brigg had no idea was available. Soon, the small house was groaning with equipment, including an electric bed for Marie, adjustable in height, with rising head and foot sections and including a sophisticated continually adjusting air mattress to reduce the possibility of pressure sores; a commode chair; a gel anti-sore cushion for chair or wheelchair; a riser-recliner chair and a hoist. Of all the equipment they would ever be presented with, this was the most daunting. It was huge, the lever arm rising in an arc up to two metres high when raised, hovering over the heavy base like a monstrous praying mantis. A contraption not unlike a robust coat hanger dangled from its mouth, large hooks on either end ready to snare the loops of the full body slings designed to cocoon the victim before lifting her away. Marie was terrified of it and refused to let it anywhere near her, but it was some time before the occupational therapist admitted defeat and gave up trying to get her to use it – including sacrificing herself to the beast in demonstration one day - and it remained squeezed into their living room, standing heavily on its castors by the wall, seemingly waiting for an opportunity to strike. By the time it was removed, Marie had started to spend an increasing amount of time in her bed and they were employing the services of a local home care provider to deal with the personal needs that Brigg was finding difficult to encompass on his own. The carers now were visiting four times a day. For a time, Brigg had been able to wheel Marie to the shower on the commode chair and then transfer her to a stool he had installed in the cubicle, but, as her muscle tone deteriorated, she found this increasingly distressing. Now, the carers would attempt to keep her clean with a bed wash each morning – with mixed success.

*There is discussion and there is argument; few are now indifferent to the session. Brigg feels vindicated. As he scans the room, he can see the fascination, the puzzlement and the disquiet that a few moments' reflection on common scientific knowledge has produced. In the course of ten minutes, they have moved from GCSE physics and biology to the most profound questions that philosophy can address. He feels it himself: just out of reach of his professional identity in the room, it is as if there is a void of unknowing dissolving away the foundations that underpin his everyday existence. He is keeping it at arm's length; his focus is the session and the students. But he wants them to feel it. It may be disconcerting, but it was important.*

At school, it had always been the science subjects; no other areas of the curriculum really interested him, except for geography - and that was because it dealt with landform, pattern and process. He had little engagement with the hosiery trade of Leicester, but he was fascinated by glaciation and geology, fluvial deposits and fossils. It had been a Catholic school, single sex and run by Jesuit priests. Naturally, religion played a significant part in the course of the school day, but by the time he was fourteen, he was so filled with questions that he began to reject it all. It became illogical, irrational and absurd, and he knew he could not continue with the naïve beliefs that had been inculcated in him since early childhood. He began to raise questions during the frequent RE lessons, known on the timetable as RD – religious doctrine, emphasising their status as the provider of cultural truth within school and their wider life as Catholics. His questions could antagonise some teachers of those lessons; this was knowledge that was not open to doubt, particularly amongst adolescents, who needed to be kept on the right path. His rejection reached a tipping point one day when he and another boy in the class had been raising some questions or objections to the focus of the lesson. Suddenly, seemingly very angry with their refusal to accept his answers, the teacher had jumped up and had started writing furiously on the board:

8 oz flour
Four eggs
6 oz sugar

8 oz butter.

Brigg and the other boy were staring at him in bewilderment. The teacher jabbed his finger furiously towards the board.

"What have I just written?" he demanded.

Brigg had been the one who had spoken.

"Er.. it looks like a recipe, sir."

The teacher glared.

"Exactly!"

Brigg had glanced at the other boy and could see he was as puzzled as he was. The teacher was waving his arms about; Brigg had never seen him quite so agitated.

"Yes," said the teacher. "A recipe. If you were making a cake, would you follow it, or would you question it?"

"I'd follow it, sir," said Brigg, a little apprehensive of this display of nervous energy.

"Yes," repeated the teacher, "you'd follow it; of course you would! You wouldn't go off and do your own thing, would you?"

"No sir."

The teacher grabbed the religious text book – Christ our Guide - from his desk and waved it at Brigg and at the rest of the class.

"This is a recipe for life. It's laid down in here what you are supposed to do and how you are supposed to live your life. It's not for picking and choosing; you have to follow it, all of it! It's not for us to select the bits we like and the bits we don't. You have to trust, just as you trust the cake recipe. The people who wrote it know the recipe works."

Shortly afterwards, Brigg stopped going to Mass on Sundays and rejected the last of the faith his parents had so wanted him to have.

Although, at O level, the scientific knowledge, like the religious, was imparted as factual and unambiguous, to be memorised for later regurgitation onto the examination paper, Brigg found it both interesting and stimulating for his young mind. For a start, its subject was nothing less than what the world is and how it works, with its focus on models and explanation providing him with a structure seemingly based on rationality not magic. Although taught as almost wholly separate subjects at that level, he began to see glimmers of how biology, physics and chemistry might be linked. For the first time, he felt there was something that vindicated his rejection of religion, the Church and what he saw as the mind-numbing incomprehensibility of worship. Here was something that gave him hope that there were answers to the burgeoning questions of his adolescent brain. As he progressed to A level and he began to cement his development of what Piaget called formal operations, the teaching of the subjects started to expand a little, allowing the beginnings of an understanding that the superficial certainties of science were also built upon provisional rather than absolute knowledge, although such doubt was more commonly encountered in the teaching of the physical sciences than within his increased focus on the biological. With higher education and his immersion in the possibilities for personal development that three years of privilege supported by the state offered, there began to emerge the realisation that all subjects are merely human divisions of the whole. Later still in life, as he transitioned to university work and studied for his PhD, he realised that no knowledge is necessarily privileged, but he still kept his love of science and did not lose the conviction that it was the models of science that could often give the quickest route to the contemplation of the eternal philosophical questions. Perhaps, he thought, they should still consider it in the curriculum as natural philosophy, for that was how and why it had arisen. It was, at least, how he now wanted his students to start to approach it, so that they might appreciate its importance in what they would be teaching.

*Brigg listens to the students' discussions for a few moments longer then gets their attention.*

*"So, it's looking as though we may have a bit of a problem. We think we can see Megan and that what we see is actually her, in physical reality. However, if we accept our scientific model, it appears that what I think I see has no physical reality in itself, but is an image in my consciousness, whatever that might be. I'm not sure what you think of that, but to me it's a bit of an issue. I want to be able to trust my senses: I want to be sure that what I perceive is really there. If I can't, how do I know the world isn't just a fabrication of my mind, like the pictures you see on your phone screen, or a hologram, or perhaps like the 3D effect you can get in an IMAX cinema? If you're sitting in the right seat, of course," he added drily.*

*The discussions start again. Holly, who had been irritated by his initial questioning, interjects again:*

*"I still think this is silly, John. Megan is causing the image I have of her: if she weren't there, I wouldn't have it, would I?"*

"Presumably not," agrees Brigg; "unless you're dreaming and are just imagining her. It's completely logical to think Megan is causing the image you have of her, but just because something seems logically correct doesn't mean that the premises for that logic are necessarily accurate."

Holly looks puzzled.

"Don't worry about that for a moment," says Brigg. "Let's explore our perception for a little longer. Why don't you shut your eyes for a moment."

Holly frowns at him. "Why?"

"Go with me on this," says Brigg. "Or, if you don't want to, how about if other people close their eyes and you watch?"

A little reluctantly, Holly closes her eyes, along with a few others in the room.

"Is Megan still there?" asks Brigg.

"Well, of course she's still there, but I just can't see her now."

"So, how do you know she's still there?"

Holly pauses, concentrating as if listening, before answering.

"If I really focused, I'd probably hear her if she'd moved."

"And can you trust your hearing?"

Holly purses her lips, thinking. Then she opens her eyes and stares at Brigg.

"Of course I can. I can hear sounds around me which tell me where things or people are. It's not as good as my sight, but I get a lot of information from my hearing."

A male student calls out from the back of the room:

"Blind people rely on their hearing much more than we do and they can develop the most amazing level of sensitivity, *more like a cat, rather than an ordinary sighted person. We can compensate if one sense goes – to an extent, at least."*

*Brigg nods. "Okay...and our hearing gives us direct access to something or someone?"*

*"Erm, well...it's sound waves isn't it, caused by the person or thing. I suppose that's direct access although it's obviously not a little bit of the person coming to our ears."*

*"So, if Megan were to make a sound, there wouldn't actually be anything of Megan in it?"*

*The student is slightly exasperated. "Well, no; it's a pressure wave, isn't it - in the air. Megan causes it and it travels through the air to our ears. Because we've got two of them we can pinpoint where the sound is coming from."*

*"And the ears?" asks Brigg. "What do they do?"*

*Amanda, the student who talked about the transmission of nerve impulses down the optic nerve, joins in. She can see where this is going.*

*"Same as the eyes, John. The eardrum turns the pressure wave into physical movement, first of the tiny ear bones and then the fluid inside the cochlea. It's then turned into nerve impulses from each ear."*

*"Which...?"*

*"Which travel.. down.. the auditory.. nerve.. to the brain..." she replies, slowly, as if reciting a doggerel. She smiles. "That then creates a sound in my consciousness."*

*Amanda looks around at her colleagues. "But it's not Megan, is it? Not really..." She frowns, thinking. "Maybe... maybe we haven't got any direct access to Megan at all."*

*More discussion. A male student sitting next to Amanda looks earnestly at her and then at Brigg.*

*"Or to anything, if you think like that... All the senses use some kind of medium and, in the end, everything is just an image in our consciousness, isn't it?"*

*Vicky, at the same table as Amanda, still looks a little confused.*

*"What about touch? Surely if I were to touch Megan, that would be direct physical contact. I'd feel her through my fingers."*

*"No you wouldn't," the male student responds; "you'd only think you did. Your nerves in your fingers send messages to the brain just like your eyes. In reality, it's all got to take place somewhere in the brain, hasn't it, John?"*

*Brigg is non-committal; he wants the students to think it through for themselves for a moment.*

*"Mmm...It's all rather strange, isn't it?*

*Megan looks up from her phone. She smiles at her friends. "And you thought you knew me..."*

He hoped he had been able to provide at least a modicum of what he saw as the proper remit of a university education within the tedium of the regimented government approach to teacher education, but it had increasingly become an uphill struggle. Increasing government control, fuelled by an ever-present media hysteria about the quality of teaching, had led to a rigorous straightjacket on initial teacher education courses. Indeed, in government eyes, it should not even be thought of as education, it was training. Teacher training, for the delivery of knowledge to pupils in school. No real questioning allowed, one had to understand the targets and deliver them. It would have been generous to imagine that there was a grand plan behind the approach, but if such a plan had been conceived it was, presumably, to produce a uniform workforce, all evenly competent, all having the same knowledge. In the end, it was Ofsted who called the shots; whatever they decided were the foci of their inspections became the dominant elements of training programmes. It didn't matter what the institution, they had to be followed, otherwise accreditation would be withdrawn. Brigg knew there were things wrong with teaching in British schools, with inconsistencies and lack of rigour in many places, but the overall result of these new policies was that British schooling and its accompanying teacher education, admired from the sixties to the nineties across the Western world for its innovation and breadth of vision, lost its spark and its raison d'etre. When Brigg had started his university career, European universities, stimulated by funding from far-sighted EU programmes such as Socrates and Erasmus, vied with each other to establish links with their British counterparts so that they could experience first-hand the progressive approaches that had been developed in UK institutions and schools. Brigg himself had been involved in a lecturer exchange with a Finnish university, travelling the length of that wonderful country. How he loved the cold, stark landscape, the thick snow blanketing the boreal pine forest, the saunas and the quiet, reserved, yet so welcoming people! Sitting naked in a conservatory open to the snow-covered forest, his body glowing with the heat of the sauna, a bottle of beer in his hand and sharing the fellowship of three other men all equally naked, yet feeling no sense of embarrassment, was an experience he would never forget. They had been good times. But slowly, the Europeans assimilated the messages in the British approach to teaching and the links dwindled. They introduced more inquiry-based strategies to their hitherto solely didactic methods and now, ironically, it was countries like Finland who were lauded as the most progressive and successful in their teaching. Britain, its creativity stifled, had lost its way.

Personally, however, he had been fortunate in his life. He had never experienced real hardship and he had managed to engineer an interesting and stimulating career for himself. He had the joy of a family and the luxury of a sound, dry, well-furnished home in whichever part of the country they had lived. Yet there was always a disquiet, always a nagging sense that there was something missing. It was not a yearning for more material comfort; it was an ever-present anguish that lay behind all his life, that sense that there was something else, something that he was missing. It wasn't a sense of purpose, but it was a sense of meaning; a feeling that just out of reach was something that would make it all make sense. He knew he was not alone in feeling this; he knew it was the burden that human beings carried that it seemed would never be assuaged. He knew that Bertrand Russell, desperate himself to understand it, had once described the sensation as 'fierce and coming from far away'. It felt like that to Brigg, too. As he got older, two antinomies began to establish themselves in his mind. A lifetime of fruitless searching for that answer had produced an acceptance that he existed in a universe that was not only not amenable to explanation, but that did not need explanation: it was as it was. He was content with that realisation. Yet with equal, but no greater, certainty, he knew there was something else, something beyond his experience and understanding that was his Theory of Everything. Both realisations vied within him in exquisite contradiction; both correct and yet wholly incompatible. He would ask himself how he could give such equal credence to both views, would linger on the contradiction for a while then shrug, and carry on.

The days turned into months and it came as a shock for Brigg to realise that Marie had been largely confined to bed for nearly a year. At first, she had still wanted to get up in the afternoons on some days and they had managed some short trips out in the car. She already qualified for help with transport through the excellent Motability scheme because of her neuropathy and they had progressed to a wheelchair accessible vehicle. This worked superbly well for a few months after they arrived, before she had taken to bed and the timetable of carer visits. They used it for short shopping trips and had managed to explore a little of the immediate area, up and down the coast. However, one day they had decided to be bold and explore the magnificent circular route via Ballachulish, Glencoe and across Rannoch moor to Bridge of Orchy, before picking up the A85 and following it back to the Pass of Brander at the foot of Cruachan and back towards Oban. In truth, it had largely been Brigg's idea and Marie had agreed to the drive without really knowing what it entailed. They had set out with excitement. The excitement was justified; the scenery was wonderful. But it had backfired spectacularly. As they turned onto the A85, with still many miles to go before home, Marie was car-sick. Brigg cursed his stupidity at undertaking a journey of such length. He stopped at the side of the road and cleaned Marie of the first bout of vomit but then drove back in a state of almost unbearable tension as, with each bend of the winding Highland road, he could see Marie's anguish as she grimaced and retched in the swaying wheelchair. Time slowed; a hundred yards became a mile. The car did not help. Upright in design, with soft French suspension, it conspired to exacerbate poor Marie's discomfort, wallowing gratuitously at every opportunity. When, finally, they had arrived home, she had been in a terrible state. Not only was her clothing covered, but the ordeal had brought out the worst in her dementia. She raged at Brigg whilst he peeled the layers of soiled clothing from her, then fought him as he tried to cleanse her face of vomit before he got her into bed. He could not change her incontinence pants before she lay down; she wouldn't let him. He made sure there were some bed pads on the mattress. Finally comfortable, she had fallen into a deep sleep and Brigg had then spent the next hour cleaning the car and putting all her clothes through the washing machine. It was the last time that Marie agreed to anything except the shortest drive.

After the initial flurry of excitement from the combined health services and the subsequent establishment of regular visits from the carers, their contact with health professionals dwindled somewhat. Although she was scheduled for monthly checks from a community nurse, these were rather spasmodic, probably because of staffing issues and the fact that as Marie was assimilated into the system she moved from being labelled acute to chronic. Such cases did not warrant the same urgency or place in the competition for scarce resources. Occasionally, Brigg raised the issue of monitoring over the telephone but as, in general, the situation was stable, he did not worry unduly at the lack of contact. It came as somewhat of a surprise to him when he was called out of the blue by a consultant to say Marie was now on his books for a visit. Apparently, she had been referred to him by the local dementia resource centre in Oban. It was his intention to visit periodically.

Brigg had been sceptical, expecting a rather perfunctory visit, but Dr. Stake had impressed from the outset. For a start, he was experienced. Whilst the nurses and other health professionals he had seen had never even heard of Primary Progressive Aphasia, Dr. Stake was well-acquainted with the condition, even if he had not had many cases himself. He was a quiet, unassuming man of about fifty, with an excellent bedside manner which put Marie at ease. After a brief, but focused examination of her, he discussed the situation with Brigg in the living room.

"How long ago was she diagnosed?" he asked.

Brigg gave a wry smile. "Nearly ten years."

He knew what Stake was going to say next.

"She's done well."

Stake looked at him searchingly, as if trying to fathom what kind of impact his statement was having.

"I know," said Brigg quietly; "defying expectations..."

Stake nodded. "Well, let's say at the upper end, anyway. She's relatively young and obviously strong, despite the CMT."

"Yes, she's been very determined all her life; she's had to be," said Brigg. "It's not until you have experience of someone with a disability, or have one yourself, that you realise just how much the world is stacked against anyone with one. She's had to battle."

The doctor agreed. "I know." He was making a few notes on a tablet computer. He finished quickly and looked up at Brigg, his voice sincere. "Life must have been hard for her."

"Well, she's always made the best of it," said Brigg, warming to Stake's apparently genuine empathy. "She's – we've – learned to anticipate and avoid, though it hasn't stopped her getting angry at the lack of awareness and imagination of most people. It's been very difficult at times. How she battled on, looking after two babies and then all the incessant action when they were toddlers, when her legs were hurting and she must have been so tired was, simply, quite remarkable. I was full of admiration for what she was doing."

"I'm sure you were," said Stake. "I've always thought that policy makers at all levels need to live in a wheelchair or immobilise a leg so they have to go around on crutches for a few months before they make decisions. It's not the big infrastructure changes that are the most important; it's those day-to-day frustrations that grind people down. Marie will have had her fair share of them, I know." He glanced down at his notes again. "And now she has this as well to contend with..."

"Yes," said Brigg ruefully; "now she has this. It's very cruel. "She didn't deserve them both."

Stake murmured in agreement. "Mmm... No, she didn't... My professional life seems to have been filled with people who have been dealt an unfair hand, through no fault of their own."

"Attitudes need to change," said Brigg. "Change the patronising approach to disability shown everywhere. Disabled people don't want pity; they just want a world that's organised in such a way that they can contribute and participate. Pitying someone never achieves anything."

"No, it doesn't," said Stake.

For a few moments, the men sat in silence. The doctor's compassion was unexpected. Marie had been the rock who had saved him from himself in their early years and who had, quite simply, become a part of his life. Why this? Why her? She had been so strong, battling her disability; this was the ultimate cruelty. She had deserved better, the prospect of an easier old age after a life of struggle. Now that would never come. It was so unfair.

Stake watched him for a few moments, leaving a silence that less sensitive people would have blundered through. Eventually, he said quietly:

"I think it will be months, not years."

Brigg breathed deeply. He was neither shocked nor surprised at the prognosis. In fact, he felt a strange wave of relief at Stake's words. Most people would tiptoe around such questions, afraid of giving bad news, afraid of causing upset. Brigg was grateful that Stake was honest; he had not asked him for a prognosis.

"You've obviously researched the condition," Stake continued, "and you know there's nothing we can do except help with management if things become difficult. She has done very well to get here; many others with PPA will not live as long."

"I know," said Brigg, nodding. He paused for a moment, then said: "The hardest thing, is that sometimes it's no longer Marie in that bed. To begin with, the decline was almost imperceptible, but now she is just slowly disappearing before my eyes." He looked straight at Stake. "Horrible to watch."

Stake gave a thin smile. "Yes, horrible, I am sure. I'm afraid that she will slowly disappear, until she lives only in your memory. Do you have family?"

Brigg explained the geographical distribution of their children and their decision to move to the Highlands whilst they could.

"Such a shame you couldn't have had more time together here."

"Well, we have to be grateful for what we have had, and what we still have," said Brigg. "I know it meant something to Marie when we moved here."

"That's good," said Stake. "And who knows what she is feeling now?" He closed his tablet, looking at his watch. "We only see outward signs of change. We go through our lives trying to decode the inner state of everyone we meet through picking up clues from their expressions and manner; but do we ever really know who's behind the eyes of the person opposite us?"

Brigg looked at him, feeling again the familiar sensation of isolation from the world. Yet this time he also felt a connection with the person talking to him. He liked Stake and was grateful for his empathy.

"No, we don't, do we?" he said slowly. "We never do..."

Stake was getting up. Brigg knew he had to move on to his next appointment; he probably had a large and pressing case load. It was not like being in a city; the next patient could be many miles away. He shook the doctor's hand.

"Thank you for your honesty."

Stake smiled. "I wish I could do more." They moved towards the door. "I'll come back in a couple of months; I'm afraid my commitments won't allow anything more."

"I understand," said Brigg, genuinely grateful that he was going to return at all. He had assumed this would be a single visit. He opened the door. Sunlight was falling on Cruachan; there was beauty in the land. As Stake stepped outside, Brigg said:

"What you said just now about the person behind the eyes: it's the great mystery, isn't it? We never know things as they are."

Stake smiled. "Life: the final frontier..." He shook Brigg's hand again. "I look forward to coming back."

When we 'see' the world, we do not see it. We process it. That glorious spring morning, when the air is filled with birdsong and the sun is shining brightly out of a clear blue sky, making the fresh green foliage so intense that the sensation almost hurts our eyes, may be just an illusion. The sounds are compression waves stimulating little hairs in our cochlea, the shimmering emerald of the trees all that is left of the light visible to our eyes that has not been absorbed by the leaves. The perceptions we experience and the sensations we feel build from electrical nerve impulses reaching our brain. Sensitivity is a wonder and a mystery, as is the consciousness that it constitutes.

It was the processing that was going wrong. Whatever was happening inside Marie had started to diverge from the normal range of responses to those stimuli from the environment. At the very heart of any relationship with another person, from a deep lifetime commitment to a momentary exchange with a passer-by, is a shared acceptance that one's fellow traveller along life's winding road is probably processing the world in much the same way as oneself. If one person is blind, or deaf, then it creates difficulties for the other side, but one learns strategies that accommodate that difference, safe in the knowledge that there is more convergence in the processing than divergence. A fine morning is still a fine morning; the nuance of the perception may vary – and it always will – but the experiences will be similar and the responses reassuringly comparable. It provides a commonality within our species and is such a normal part of everyday communication that it is truly disturbing when we encounter someone who does not, apparently, share our impressions.

We expect predictability. Marie was becoming less and less predictable in her responses, to everything. A beautiful sunrise over the hills could just as likely be met with a grunt as delight, as could the presence of people, including Brigg. This unpredictability could be disconcerting and sometimes aggressive. At those times, he had to fight hard to quell his instinctive urge to leap verbally to his own defence and it took a little while before he managed to accommodate these mood swings without experiencing a sense of affront. This was not Marie; the part of her neural processing that held the core of the old Marie together was eroding away. There were gaps everywhere. When Brigg could distance himself from the immediate, defensive response to her outbursts, the gaps were obvious. He wondered what it must be like on the inside; so often, it appeared to be distressing.

It had been a good night. Marie had slept right through, which meant that Brigg did too. She was awake now; he could hear her making quiet, rhythmical sounds as she breathed, as if humming. They were not sounds of distress, but they definitely indicated that she was moving steadily into wakefulness and that Brigg would need to get up very soon. It was a quarter to six. He pulled the duvet back and sat up on the side of their new bed; even though it was now just for him, he tended to stay on one side. As the weeks and months progressed, he began to stretch out across what had become a vast potential space for sleeping, but it had felt strange. Nearly forty years of sharing a bed had developed a primeval nesting instinct to sleep in the same place. The other side was hers, not his.

Regardless of whether Marie was awake, he knew he had to be up. The carers would be coming sometime after seven thirty and in the intervening time he had to wash, dress and get his breakfast, then organise Marie's, along with administering her medications and cleaning her teeth, when she was amenable. Sometimes all went smoothly, sometimes he was left drained by half past seven after battling against her blank refusal to comply with anything. The pills would stay on the side and he would try later; the bowl of cereal or marmite on toast were thrown away. He was tired. This was every day; there were no days off. Some days, he wondered how long he could continue.

After a brief trip to the bathroom, he dressed, then went into her room to open her curtains and raise her bed so that she could see out to their front garden and what was a potentially wonderful view across the loch towards Cruachan. Marie did not look at him, but continued to make low humming noises as she looked out at the hills.

"Just getting my breakfast," he said as cheerily as he could. "I'll be back in ten minutes."

He said the same every day.

He ate his breakfast in the kitchen. Toast and marmalade; he never varied. Whilst the toast was in, he prepared her cereal, poured her a drink and pressed the tablets out of their bubbles into an eyebath he used as a medication pot. She had three types of medication: a mood stabiliser, a 75mg aspirin tablet to keep her blood thin and to diminish the risk of stroke and some vitamin D, because now she was bed bound, she had little exposure to sunlight. Stake had suggested to him to alternate the pills; today was a mood stabiliser and an aspirin.

As Marie had taken to her bed, the walls had closed in for him too. He could no longer leave the house. Sometimes the irony was extreme. With all the beauty of the hills around him and the promise of the culmination of his lifelong desire to live somewhere he could roam free in the wild grandeur, he was confined to one place. The most he could do was to potter in the garden whilst she was asleep, gazing across the loch, his imagination searching for the solitude of the high corries and the rough ground of the peaks. The frustration had become a part of his daily existence. Most times, it was only a dull ache in the background of his everyday routines, assuaged a little when he found the excuse to take the opportunity of the carers' visit to walk the three hundred yards to the post box, drinking in the fresh air as he stretched his limbs and smelling the salty odour of seaweed coming from the loch. But, when the sun shone and the sky was clear with the sparkling freshness that only the west coast could provide, it could be too much and he would find himself weeping as he walked, his body bursting with a desperate longing to be elsewhere. In those times, only his imagination and his ability to look inward and detach himself from the transience of external reality could save him from despair. But it was hard and he could feel himself being drawn into a growing resentment. Such thoughts filled him with remorse and he knew how devastated he would be if – when - she should die, but still they came, when his energy was low and his self-pity strong.

The extent of his turmoil could be exemplified by his response to the many offers of respite help he had received from the care company and other local organisations, not to mention their kind neighbours, a couple their age living about sixty yards down the road. They had made them feel welcome from the moment they moved in, unperturbed that they were incomers from the south, offering help in whatever form they wanted. The man, Angus, owned a fishing boat on the loch and he had begun to bring them the occasional mackerel, pollack or even small cod. Brigg fancied that it gave him an excuse to visit but he enjoyed his warm, good-humoured company. Angus, like the carers, kept reiterating that he, or his wife Flora, would be very happy to sit with Marie whilst Brigg took the opportunity to get out for an hour, but Brigg found it difficult to think about leaving her with strangers for that length of time. Once, when the carers were there and he had tarried just a little on a walk down to the post box, she had become aware that he was no longer in the house. By the time he had returned, she was agitated. It had taken some time for her to calm. Brigg knew then that, despite all the kind offers, he could not, as yet, countenance leaving her for an extended period. Besides, if he were honest, he knew that he would not be able to relax if he left her with strangers, so there would be little point in going anyway. Her fate was his fate.

He knew something was wrong as soon as he came back with her breakfast. She was still making the strange humming noises, seemingly lost in her own world. In order to help her, to give her pills or to help her eat, he would sometimes have to spend time gaining her attention. Not this morning. As he came back into her room, she was staring at him, her eyes wide. He knew the look and it did not bode well.

He tried to ignore it, placed her bowl of cereal and a milk bottle on the bedside table and took the pot with the pills in it. He held it out towards her mouth.

"Do you want to take these?" he said, calmly.

The swipe with the hand and the shout were simultaneous.

"No!"

It was one of the few words that she still could articulate.

The pills flew across the room as her hand connected with his. He placed the pot out of her reach and went to pick them up. He brushed the dust off them..

"Do you want to try again?" he said calmly, proffering it again.

Her arm shot out again, but this time he was ready. He moved his hand away. Her eyes were still staring and now her mouth was contorted with an inexplicable anger. She had few words left, but emotion could make her find them.

"You!"

He backed away; he knew what was coming.

"What's that for?" he asked as calmly as he could. His frustration was rising; he knew the carers would be coming fairly soon and he wanted to get this done. There was still her breakfast. He moved his hand towards her one last time, with little hope of success.

He was met by a snarl; her eyes were wild. She was trying to say something and a torrent of unintelligible angry sounds came from her mouth, interspersed with a repeated "You!", as if accusing him of something. She was getting flushed.

The pills went back in the pot; he would try again later. He searched his mind, trying to think what the trigger might have been. He held up the bowl of cereal.

"I don't suppose you want any of this, do you?"

She stared angrily and started shouting at him again. He stepped back, picking up the milk. He tried to keep his voice calm and matter of fact, even though he could feel a rising frustration on the verge of anger at her at the irrationality of it all. He looked her directly in the eyes and said firmly:

"Don't talk to me like that; I don't deserve it."

She bared her teeth. He turned to the door.

"Okay, I'm not staying here whilst you behave like this. Scream and shout as much as you like but I'm not coming back now until you stop. You can take it out on the carers; they'll be here soon."

He walked out of the room and pulled the door closed behind him. He could hear her continue to rant as he took the bowl and milk back to the kitchen. He'd left the pills in the room for later. He was getting better at managing his response to these mood swings. When they had started, he would spend time trying to talk her down, knowing that her dementia precluded rational intervention, but driven to try. It was so illogical; surely he could get through to her? It was, of course, a fruitless activity, achieving nothing except to exacerbate his own feelings of distress and helplessness. Where was this anger coming from? It was only when he saw that she would also direct her anger at the carers or anyone else who happened to be close, that he steeled himself to change his approach. This was the dementia talking; the Marie that he knew was no longer in the room. But it was hard to change; every instinct was rebelling at the infuriating irrationality of her behaviour and it took a great effort of will for him to detach himself from his emotional response and his intellectual frustration. He watched how the carers treated her and was envious. They had no emotional connection and they let her outbursts wash over them, getting on with their job of administering personal care professionally and admonishing her forcefully if she would try to stop them. It was as if they were treating a young child. His first reaction had been one of indignation: this was Marie, not a child, treat her with respect! This was the kind of treatment that got care homes a bad name, slowly stripping residents of their dignity. But, by the time he had endured a few of these swings, he realised they were right. He had to detach the behaviour from his concept of Marie. This was a different person. If this person was acting like a two-year-old, then she had to be treated as such. You don't try to reason with a two-year-old having a tantrum. It began to work. Now, as he poured the dry cereal back into the packet, he could hear her ranting start to subside a little. He wouldn't go back in until after the carer's visit. She could miss breakfast today; it wouldn't matter, and he would try the pills later on.

By the time the carers came, Marie was quiet again. He told them what had happened and they suggested they try with the medication. Brigg smiled wryly to himself; he knew what would happen, and it did. She took the pills without a murmur. When they had finished with her pad change and bed bath, one of them presented him with a bag containing her soiled pad. She smiled. "Bowel movement." There was always a trigger somewhere and how uncomfortable it must be to lie in a soiled pad! Moreover, there was the indignity; a part of Marie could still feel the rage at such a situation. Brigg took the bag and disposed of it, feeling wretched that he'd been tempted to be angry with her. How ghastly that must be. When the carers left, Marie slept.

Brigg went out into the front garden and stood on their small area of grass, looking over the loch towards the mountains. The clouds were beginning to lift; it promised to be good weather later on. He breathed in the fresh, clean air, letting his mind grow calm and expand away from the confines of the house. A lifetime's experience of the hills and lochs, real or imagined, and a deep love of the minutiae of the landscape, allowed him to place himself in the midst of the hills whilst still rooted to the little patch of ground surrounding their cottage. There was a faint scent of seaweed; the tide must be ebbing. All the sheltered sea lochs had rich growths of knotted wrack around their shores and, as the tide ebbed, great mats of trailing brown algae would become evident. At high water, this plant rose high in the water column, buoyed by its large air bladders, its extensive fronds often reaching a metre in length. Brigg remembered his times as a student exploring the wonderful communities of creatures living amongst the algal forests of rocky shores and sheltering in the tangled fingers of the holdfasts; his year's specialism in marine ecology had been a highlight of his degree programme. As the tide fell, these fronds would carpet the rocks, making any attempt to walk through them almost impossible, but providing cool, damp shelter to myriad unseen organisms waiting for the return of the sea. Even during the hot days of high summer, when the sun would dry the upper fronds until they were crisp and apparently dead, it was always wet in the depths beneath, where winkles, topshells, whelks, anemones, starfish, crabs, blennies, polyps, sponges, worms and too many other creatures to list, were safe from whatever the weather chose to do. That was one of the great fascinations of shoreline ecology for him; hiding in plain sight was a whole world of life, unseen and unknown to all but the dedicated naturalist. It had fired his imagination, giving him an outlet when times were difficult and the world had begun to close in. It was also whilst he was a student that he had begun to develop the ability to project himself into these places, losing himself in imagined rock pools and barnacle-covered cliff faces, or steep montane slopes with their crags offering precarious hospitality to wild, twisted rowans and their tumbling streams feeding sphagnum-rich bogs and grasslands. As his familiarity with these landscapes grew, he could make himself hear the cries of ravens and buzzards, those wonderfully evocative sounds of solitude. Now, as he could do no more than patrol his little piece of earth's surface in and around the cottage, this ability to dream was his lifeline.

When Marie woke, the cloud had passed. She lay quietly in bed, half-watching an old television that he had installed on a table alongside her bed. There was no aerial point in the dining room, so he had rigged an extension from the sitting room, with a high cable now hanging like a washing line across the hall to her bedroom. He knew how the day would go from here. Once she woke, she would lie patiently for an hour or so, with the monotony of daytime television droning quietly in the background, drifting in and out of sleep, until the carers returned around twelve to half past. Then he would get her lunch of boiled egg, some crackers or oatcakes with small pieces of smoked salmon or ham as well as a little cheese, accompanied by a banana and a segmented clementine. Sometimes she wanted a little more, sometimes she refused it all. It had ceased to worry him. Overall, she was still eating and, more importantly, she was still drinking reasonably well. He knew that refusal to drink was the danger sign. After the carers came at lunchtime, there were a few hours until their next visit at about four-thirty, then he would produce a hot meal of sorts and they would have a couple of hours together watching early evening television before the carers returned for their last pad change at eight, settling her for the night. That was her day, and his. It was all very predictable.

As the daily routine had been imposed on his own life, he had railed against the mind-numbing monotony of each day, characterising his situation as akin to house arrest. It felt as though he was wasting life; who knew how much he had left himself? Each day, he looked out to the now unreachable hills across the loch. That was when he needed all his powers of imagination to keep his emotions calm. But he could not stop himself anticipating a time when he might have the freedom to explore. He bought maps online and began to plan climbs and walks, even wondering whether to buy a small boat like Angus and take some trips up the loch. But at the same time as he indulged in this planning, he was also riddled by guilt. It was as if he was wishing Marie gone. His emotions became a battleground between forces of loyalty and responsibility and his yearning for time to himself. The result was a deep angst that was never far from his consciousness. From deep within him, he could feel the last vestiges of his Catholic upbringing stirring, accusing him of being a bad person intent only on his own selfish desires. They had been difficult days.

Yet slowly, the angst subsided and he began to find something strangely liberating about adapting to the routine. One day had become the same as the last and would be the same as the next. The routine of getting up at the same hour each morning and the cycle of carers' visits punctuated the day, along with the discipline of mealtimes and even the structures of phrases and sentences as he interacted with the woman who had been his wife of forty years and whom he still loved with all his heart. Hours sped by; the morning-time when she slept and he had a little space to do essential jobs in the house or garden went by in a flash and, almost before he realised it, he would be planning the evening meal. Then, a whisky and bed. Repeat. Repeat. Day, evening, sleep; day, evening, sleep. He was reminded of the description given by H. G. Wells' Time Traveller as he piloted his Time Machine, of how he saw the days speed up: day, then night; day...night; day, night; day night; light, dark; light dark; until they merged into a grey as the Machine sped into the future, with the Traveller himself standing outside time. It was engulfing him, yet as he focused on the way it was obliterating his normal life, he began to realise that he was not lost within the monotony. Slowly, it was becoming merely a backdrop, a pattern against which he existed in a life that continued outside, or at least alongside, this basic regularity. For the first time in his life, he began to understand the attraction of the closed lives of monasteries and communities the world over. Monotony and predictability could liberate rather than enslave.

Time is a fabrication, a construction of the human mind. That naïve conception of past and future, so central to our understanding of our existence and so fundamental to the way we plan our lives, is an illusion. There is no past, there is no future; there is only now. What we experience as time is an unfolding, continuous present. We do not travel into the future; we create it as we live. Whether that is the true reality of existence, we cannot know and, indeed, the question is irrelevant. It is all that we have; it is, as far as we know, all we will ever have. The illusion of time blankets existence in uniformity; uniformity of duration, uniformity of travel. But we know that cannot be. Since Einstein we have known it does not apply in physics and a brief reflection suggests that our everyday time differs from moment to moment, person to person, species to species. It is impossible to know whether the way one experiences time is the same as one's neighbour and it is certainly different from the way one's cat gets through its day. For a spider, there is simply existence; stretches of nothing but static readiness interspersed by explosions of being. As his confinement proceeded, Brigg began to understand that his unfolding moment, although emotionally and intellectually bound to his history and his desires, was not dependent on them. He was dependent neither on place nor activity, no matter how strong his longing for certain experiences might be. As this realisation grew, so did his acceptance of the uniformity of his everyday life, even though some urges were so deep they would never completely be assuaged.

For the spider, once her web is made, time stops. She is, but she could just as easily be is not. Not for her the frenetic activity of the fly about to trigger her next moment of life. Waiting is a human conception. It implies anticipation and control. The spider does not wait; until the fly blunders into the unseen silken threads and transmits its frantic struggles into movement in the spider's limbs, she is not waiting. She is not. There is no time at all. Her time depends on sensation.

Perhaps, Brigg wondered, all time does.

*Megan stretches in her chair.*

*"You can finish now, if you'd like," says Brigg. "Thank you for being the guinea pig; you've been the perfect focus. Although, of course" he adds with a smile, standing a red board marker upright on the table in front of him, "this board marker would probably have done the job. Just not as big."*

*Megan wrinkles her nose. "Oh, thanks for the compliment, John!"*

*Brigg laughs. "My pleasure! Anyway," he says in an exaggerated tone, "you have made an invaluable contribution to the session – and pushed back the boundaries of human understanding."*

*Megan grunts in satisfaction. "That's better; that's exactly what I thought I was doing."*

*She joins her friends, smiling at them as she sits down.*

*Brigg looks at the students. The unfocused group that had started the session is no longer there: nearly all of them now look lively and interested. The sun is slipping behind the flats and the November chill is descending on the campus outside; all eyes are now turned inwards. He feels relaxed. He is happy with where the session is going.*

*"Okay," he continues, "so perhaps we do have a problem. If everything is an image in our consciousness, how can we be certain about what we are seeing, despite what we think we perceive from our senses?"*

*Amanda purses her lips, as if concentrating on a thought.*

*"I agree it's rather disconcerting, John, but surely there's something inside us that* knows *something exists? Just because our senses work in that way doesn't mean to say it doesn't."*

*"Of course not," agrees Brigg. "However, whether it does or not is one of the central problems of philosophy. It makes us think about the difference between sensation and perception,*

*and between perception and reality. Is what we think we 'see' of the world supported by the sensory input we receive, or do we make it up – constructing it, as we might say? The question is almost as old as Western philosophy itself. In modern terms, we sometimes think of it as a tension between materialism, the idea that a physical external world exists that we have access to, and idealism, which suggests that ultimately there is no solid, external reality at all: it is an illusion generated by our minds – or even, perhaps, by a single entity that we could just call Mind."*

*He could see that Amanda is going to come back at him with another question, as are some others. He holds up his hand.*

*"I know it might be frustrating, but we can't go much further with that right now," he says, apologetically. "Some of you would get cross with me, with good reason. Yes, of course it all concerns science education, and underpins all the deliberations of the philosophy of science, but it's too involved for this short module. What I want to encourage you to do is to think hard about what we mean by observation: that central plank of scientific method that we always say is the most important feature to develop in young children. Be questioning about it. I think we may be a little guilty of oversimplification; we talk about children's observation 'skills', as if we can simply fine tune them to some pre-set perfection and then they will see what's really there. But maybe it's a little more complex than that. What kind of knowledge does observation give us? Does anyone just observe, or are you thinking all the time when you're observing, so in fact you're constructing your observations as you make them? If we are, how objective is the knowledge our observation gives us? Of course, you're not*

*going to talk to young children in those terms, and it is fundamentally important that you encourage them to develop the ability to focus clearly on the world, but knowing something of the complexity within the development you are promoting is the job of the teacher. It allows you to deal with the unexpected response, the difficult question. You may want to explore the ideas the children are bringing to their observations and it will make you comfortable with allowing wonder and inquiry. Otherwise, you are just an automaton in the classroom: the government might as well employ robots." Brigg smiles at the group. "And that idea's not as far-fetched as it might sound; there are some who think that educational purposes might be better served by that kind of teaching. If they ever develop usable artificial intelligence, watch out." He waves his hand dismissively at them. "Many politicians think that a more rigidly controlled approach would produce much better results, rather than have them sullied by you lot and all your different agendas and political ideals..."*

*The baying for university programmes to be shut down and for teachers to 'learn on the job' in schools was getting louder. Unless they fought hard, they'd be gone in ten years...*

*"For those of you who want to go deeper into the bigger questions of materialism and idealism, you'll find that in Western thought they go back at least as far as the Ancient Greek philosophers like Aristotle and Plato, and there has been much speculation from the Enlightenment period of the eighteenth century onwards. If you feel the urge to get up to speed with a general overview of important philosophical ideas, you could do worse than read Bertrand Russell's 'A History of Western Philosophy'. It's a bit old now, and Russell isn't to everyone's taste, but it does give a fascinating*

*panorama of three thousand years of thinking. It will take you from the ancient Greeks to the middle of the twentieth century – and you can always dip in rather than read it straight. There's also an excellent novel called 'Sophie's World', by a Norwegian called Jostein Gaarder. It deals with the same questions, has the same general overview as Russell and is a lot more entertaining! Some of you may know it. I wish that our modules were long enough for us to be able to address these big philosophical questions in more detail, but," he smiled mischievously, "for some reason, you've got to cover things like ICT and PE as well. Never mind!"*

*The plan for the rest of the session is crystallising in Brigg's mind.*

*"What I'd like to do for the rest of this afternoon is try to consolidate a little about what we think we know about our senses." He scans the room, pleased that the students seem happy to go along with him. "For starters, then, where did they come from?"*

*"What do you mean, John?" one of them asks.*

*Brigg realises he's asked the wrong question. "Ok, let's look at it another way. Why do we have sense organs at all?"*

*The student who had shown he was beginning to appreciate the paradoxical nature of sensory understanding, calls out in a rather dismissive tone:*

*"That's fairly obvious, John, isn't it? Just like all animals, it's so we can interact in the world: catch food, keep safe from predators."*

*"Find a mate..." suggests another, to smiles across the group.*

*A female student at the back suggests: "Everything needs to know what's going on around it, otherwise it will just get eaten."*

*"Sensitivity – it's one of the seven life processes," says another. "It's one way you know something's alive not dead."*

*"Very good," says Brigg, in mock praise; "we'll make biologists of you yet. So do all animals have eyes?"*

*"Yeah, I suppose so," says a student called Becky who hasn't yet contributed to the session. "Even insects have some kind – those complex ones."*

*"Compound," corrects someone at her table.*

*"Yeah, that's it."*

*"Earthworms, Becky?" asks Brigg.*

*"Er... well, no." Becky looks around for support. "They don't, do they?"*

*"But they're animals, aren't they?"*

*Becky looks rather flummoxed. She answers hesitantly:*

*"Well...yes...are they?"*

*Brigg never ceases to be surprised at the lack of understanding of the term 'animal'. All the students will have GCSE science and some will have taken a science subject at A level. It had come to signify a concept comprised almost exclusively of mammals, the smaller and more furry the better. A recent television fundraising campaign by no less than the RSPCA had claimed they were committed to 'saving all animals'. Brigg had wondered if he ought to call them regarding his pet cockroach...*

*"So, have they got eyes?" he asks again.*

*She frowns.*

*"No, of course not."*

*"So, what would you say if I told you it's been shown they are sensitive to light? They will move away from a light source. Obviously, that's useful if you want to live under the ground. But how do they do that if they haven't got eyes?"*

*Becky shrugs helplessly. "I don't know...maybe they sort of feel it."*

*Brigg smiles supportively; he doesn't want to undermine her confidence. "That's actually a very interesting idea – what, like heat?"*

*Becky looks around at her colleagues for help.*

*"Yeah...possibly," she says tentatively.*

*Help arrives from another part of the room.*

*"Don't they have light sensitive cells somewhere? I seem to remember something about that at A level."*

*"What, like eyes but only tiny ones?"*

*"Yeah. Something like that, but really simple. They must have, mustn't they? There's got to be something there; they've got to pick it up somehow. They can't be seeing with their whole body."*

*"Can't they? Why not?"*

*Becky concurs. "That's just silly, John; nothing goes round with its whole body as an eye. Ben must be right; it's got to be something like light sensitive cells."*

*"But I thought you said they might just be able to feel it, like heat."*

*"Well, it's sort of the same, isn't it?" Becky's lack of understanding is making her a little irritable. "Stop playing games, John. Is that's what it's like?"*

*Brigg smiles. "Ok, yes, Ben is right; they have a lot of light sensitive cells, dotted all over their bodies, but with a concentration at the head end. Obviously, they're not eyes as we imagine them and we probably should be careful of talking about an earthworm 'seeing'. But they're certainly sensitive to light. The cells are called ocelli; it sounds different, but it just means little eyes in Latin. Biologists love to do that sort of thing when they're thinking of a name for something that's similar to something else but different."*

*"Just bloody confusing, I'd say. So they don't have eyes, but they do really."*

*Brigg laughs. "Yeah, I suppose so, just very simple. There are usually a few special cells working together to receive the light, so it's not just a single cell, though you'll find other organisms that seem to work right down at that level too. They are not complex enough to be called an organ, as vertebrate eyes are, because that would imply a combination of tissues."*

*"Or octopus eyes," another student suggests.*

*"Good point. Those are fascinating. Members of the octopus family have eyes that are very similar in structure to vertebrate eyes."*

*Brigg realises he is short on visual examples to help them understand what he means. A disadvantage of working off the cuff.*

*"Sorry, I should have a couple of images for you to see. If you don't know what I'm talking about and can't visualise an octopus eye, have a look later, if you're interested. You'll see what I mean. Not now..." he adds quickly, as some immediately get out their mobile phones to start searching; "just go with the idea and look at the examples later. It's not important at this moment."*

*He moves on quickly. A few students continue searching, but he ignores them.*

*"The important point is that sensitivity to light energy actually seems to be fundamental to all forms of life. In fact, Becky, maybe your idea of being able to feel it like heat isn't so far-fetched. In order to understand, we have to suspend our intuitive understanding, because that's the only way we have a chance of understanding what might really be happening. One thing one learns about science is that if an explanation feels intuitively right, it's quite possibly wrong.*

*"As humans, using our eyes to see is so second nature to most of us that we assume our version of 'seeing' is what sensitivity to light means. We interpret everything else we see around us in terms of our own experience. Why? Why is our way of experiencing the only one, or the right one? The tendency to think like that does two things: it blinds us to other possible ways of sensing and making sense of the world and it makes us arrogant. It makes us think we have a privileged perspective: the best version of life. It makes us think we are at the pinnacle and it permeates our common evolutionary understanding of the structure of the living world. But take eyes: there seems to be a general principle that more complex organisms tend to have more complex structures, but it's not always the case. Octopus eyes are one example and we would normally consider molluscs to be rather primitive. Much more primitive than molluscs, however, we have lots of other examples. I'm sure you've heard of box jellyfish, those highly dangerous tropical cnidarians that you have to be careful of if you go swimming in the sea around Australia and some other places. Their sting can kill you. You'd think, being jellyfish, they would be very primitive and I suppose they are, but actually they've got ocelli that also seem to have a rudimentary lens and retina. Maybe, the basic pattern of how animals were*

*going to process light efficiently emerged quite early on in evolutionary terms. Given that our cameras are pretty similar, maybe there isn't any other kind of structure that would work."*

*He scans the group. He knows that there is a flourishing Christian society on the university campus and that it is likely that some of the students may belong to it. Over recent years, these societies had begun to be influenced by the evangelical ideas coming out of the fundamentalist Christian movement in the United States, along with the ignorant critique of science that it promoted. These evangelical groups were very active on social media, and particularly influential amongst susceptible young people. It was quite possible that at least some of the group would be holding ambivalent ideas about evolution, or even reject it. He needs to choose his words carefully. He doesn't want to annoy them, but he needs to make a point. He continues:*

*"Now, I know that some people have reservations about evolution on religious grounds. It's not my job to tell them they are wrong, although you can probably tell that I think they are. However, what is my job is to help you to have a good grounding in accepted scientific ideas and why those ideas are deemed to be worth taking seriously. These are science sessions and evolution is a part of the accepted framework of understanding that science brings to an explanation of the world. You should by now have a good understanding of the way that science works and why we can place a strong degree of trust in scientific ideas. Science produces reliable knowledge. No-one can claim it is true; I'm afraid no-one has access to truth, whatever that might mean. All human knowledge is provisional and it is always liable to modification and change. What we should look for, and what science insists on, is*

*knowledge that is robust and withstands challenge and critique. Yes, I want you to remain critical, but being critical is more complex than saying 'I don't believe that'. There are criteria for how you should decide whether something is worth accepting; it's not just a matter of whim, and I'm afraid it's more complex than saying it's not found in the Scriptures. The first place you should employ your critical thinking is with anyone, and I mean* anyone, *who professes to know the 'truth'. That, to me, includes religious belief, although I'm sure some might disagree."*

*Brigg scans the room, looking for a reaction. Most are listening calmly, but he can see he has touched a nerve with a few that he could predict, like Holly. She is frowning. He carries on; if he can make her be a little circumspect about what she believes, he would consider he had been successful. Of course, he will probably never know.*

*"The idea inherent in the theory of evolution that human beings have not been specially created but that they developed from other, less human animals, has always offended some people, largely on religious grounds, but also because it challenges our innate sense of superiority. A major sticking point with many has always been the length of time required for evolution to take place in the way it is suggested; it needs hundreds of millions of years. But what's the problem? I would suggest to you that if you can conceive of yesterday and the day before that, there is no logical reason not to conceive of a hundred days before, a thousand, a million or in fact millions of years. One implies the other: if you can have a lifetime of yesterdays, and I've had fifty-five years of them, why shouldn't they have always been there? However, some, such as the Creationists, reject the possibility of such a large time span;*

*they think that the world is only about six thousand years old, basing their ideas, it would seem, on the four-hundred-year-old claims of an Irish bishop." Brigg raised his eyebrows. "Apparently, if you add up all the generations in the Bible, you end up with the world being made on the 23rd October, four thousand and four BC. ... They also believe that every species was put on the Earth fully formed. Such thinking has been discredited on many levels, from rational scientific critique to Biblical scholarship, but, as I know many people seem to be convinced by it, or maybe," he suggests, catching a few students' quizzical expressions, "feel the tension between it and evolutionary ideas, we have to acknowledge that it is there and increasingly present in common discourse, for example on social media, where you will find just about any idea you can think of, true or not."*

*He's gone much further than he intended. Once he had started talking, his irritation with what he saw as the mindless, but dangerous, ideas of the Christian right had propelled him into a much more involved exposition. He needs to focus again. This was not the point of the session.*

*"As we're talking about eyes, however, I'd like to draw your attention to one of the arguments often put forward by Creationists. They say that eyes are so complex, they could not have developed slowly, in incremental steps. They will ask: 'What use is half an eye? You need a whole one to work'. Well, I would suggest that looking in more detail shows just how misguided such questions are. For a start, as Richard Dawkins has often pointed out, if half an eye still gave me an idea of something going on around me, it's definitely of some use. It may not focus well like a 'whole eye', or perhaps see in colour, but it might still tell me when there is some movement that*

*could be a predator, or something to eat. Actually, however, the 'half-eye' argument completely misses the point regarding evolution. What Dawkins has also asked us to do is conceive of an eye that is just a bit less efficient than the ones we have now. It would still give a huge amount of information to the organism that has it and provide the behavioural advantages that would suggest it would be selected for. Then you go back another step, and another. Dawkins calls it climbing Mount Improbable. Although there may be times that evolution has happened in broad leaps – 'saltation' as it's called – most is thought to proceed in these very gradual ways. That's where the necessity for vast spans of time becomes obvious, and if you can't accept that, I can see you would have difficulties.*

*"When you look in detail at animal cells and tissues, you begin to see that light sensitivity appears to be fundamental to living things. From simple cellular responses, through more complex aggregations of cells in primitive ocelli to the differentiation of tissues in eyes like ours, you can see that a light response seems to be ubiquitous – it's everywhere. Of course, that's not just animals; plants, as we know, are sensitive to light, and not just for photosynthesis. You could argue that earthworm ocelli are examples of the 'half-eyes' of the Creationists, and they are definitely of some use to the earthworm. To my mind, evolution is the only satisfactory way of explaining how we have the graduated complexity that we see today in the animal kingdom. In the end, I have to leave it to you to decide for yourself what you think, but please make those decisions on the firmest, most rational of arguments and not just those which might seem intuitively appealing or that give you a warm fuzzy feeling. Human life," he added ruefully, "seems to be about reconciling rationality with that warm*

*fuzziness, but you can only do that by embracing and interrogating both, not by ignoring one at the expense of the other."*

*The students are quiet. "Close your eyes for a moment."*

*He waits until most of them have complied. "Now," he continues; "is the light still falling on your body?"*

*There is a murmur of affirmation.*

*"What's happening to it?"*

*"It's bouncing off, like we said about seeing Megan," one student suggests.*

*"And also being absorbed," adds another. "It's always being absorbed; that's what we were saying about seeing colours, it's the wavelengths that haven't been absorbed that give us the experience of colour."*

*"Exactly," says Brigg. "Is your body using the light it's absorbed?"*

*Hesitation. One says tentatively: "No... not with my eyes shut."*

*"No, that's not right, Fi" objects Ben, his eyes screwed tightly, as if he is trying hard to feel for the light through his skin. "I suppose it still is using it, though not to see with. I was trying to imagine lying out on a beach with my eyes shut, feeling the sun on my body. I'm feeling warm, that's heat and I'm also going red, or tanning. That's my cells reacting to the light falling on them."*

*"That's not light; that's ultraviolet."*

*"It's still light; just another part of the spectrum. And anyway, can't butterflies see using the ultraviolet?"*

*Fiona is indignant.*

*"That's cheating, Ben; it's not what we think of as light. All the visible light is useless to us with our eyes closed."*

*"Yeah, but that's only our idea of visible, Fi; butterflies would object."*

*Fiona scowls. "Oh, don't be ridiculous, Ben. We all know what we mean by visible light."*

*Ben shrugs. "Well, maybe we're wrong. What isn't visible is only a different wavelength of electromagnetic radiation. Also, when you think about it, there might be millions of animals that use light for getting about, but not in the same way as us. Evolution has taken the vertebrates in a certain direction and concentrated the sense organs at the front end. Lots of other animals that don't move like us have them all over their bodies. That's right, John, isn't it?"*

*Brigg nods in agreement. "Yep; starfish have light sensitive cells on the ends of their arms, scallops have lots dotted round the mantle just under the shell, so they are sensitive to movement all round when they're resting on the sea bed. But for animals that move in one direction, there seems to have been an evolutionary pressure to concentrate light sensitivity at the end that moves forward. For example, many flatworms have a couple of what are called eyespots at the front end, and they are relatively very simple creatures – although, of course, just about anything living is actually a complex structure."*

*Fiona is still doubtful. She frowns. "Yeah, but that just makes them like us; they're not seeing with their bodies. It's not an argument."*

*Brigg smiles. "Good point, but actually wrong in this case. Amazingly, it seems that flatworms can see with the rest of their body as well."*

*"In that case, why have they got eyes at all?"*

*Brigg laughs.*

*"Fair question. The answer, I think, lies in what I was saying a minute ago. We've got to stop thinking that light sensitivity only means seeing in the way that we do. It makes sense for animals like us and the rest of the vertebrates, and perhaps octopi and spiders and all those animals with highly developed complex eyes that we know might have the potential to help form some kind of image; there are the associated structures and nervous system to be able to process and use the information. However, if you take a much more simple organism such as a flatworm, it's likely that being sensitive over their whole body wouldn't be as confusing as we might imagine. We're not talking about images; we're dealing with responses to stimuli which can affect their overall behaviour. It can stimulate them to move towards or away from light sources, much as plants grow towards the sun. Our intuitive human perspective can skew our thinking. We need to be careful about talking of images. From what we were saying earlier, an image is something that is formed in our consciousness. It's not a 'thing' that we could see by looking at the animal. Are flatworms conscious? Somehow, I doubt it."*

*Brigg pauses. What is this life he experiences? He is aware of a sea of faces looking at him; faces that he is creating. A shudder of infinite loneliness fills him. From out of the void comes the slow, incessant beat of the timeless question of his life. It is there, just as it has always been there, and he is no nearer an answer that he has ever been.*

*He makes himself continue. "A fascinating feature is that it seems the worm can differentiate between the two sources of stimulation."*

*Talking centres him again, the loneliness receding. He smiles at the students. "Imagine you're a flatworm, trundling along the bottom in a lake. It's all a bit gloomy down there. Your eyespots are giving you an indication of what's in front of you, but at the same time, your whole body is responding to lighter and darker areas around you. Patterns of shade and brightness as you move past things. Perhaps, your body is programmed to move towards dark areas if you're threatened; it might be a crevice where you can hide. You only have a very simple nerve structure, even in comparison with earthworms, but what you've got has concentrations of cells which appear to have some form of central processing function, enabling you to respond differently and preferentially to the two sources of information."*

*The question becomes suffused with a warmth of acceptance. This is his life; it is full and it is fascinating, as much as it is absurd and inexplicable. The answer is either in him or it exists elsewhere; better to feel the question, than never to feel it at all.*

*He smiles. "You're actually much more sophisticated than you might think – if you could think at all. What fun it is being a flatworm!"*

*Laughter.*

*"Tests have shown that you can at times override the general sensitivity and respond solely to the information coming from your eyespots. As I said, we're not talking about seeing in the way that we do; these are probably in the order of stimulus-response reflexes, but even these responses are extraordinarily complex, promoting all sorts of possible behavioural changes."*

*Brigg laughs with the students. "It's seeing, Jim, but not as we know it..."*

*He adds:*

*"I haven't a clue how you test the nervous functioning of flatworms, just as I also don't understand how you investigate quantum particles. But that doesn't mean that I don't accept the findings. These findings are written up in peer-reviewed papers and that's how science works: with diligence, critique and integrity, and when it doesn't it justifiably leads to outrage. You've probably heard about the scandal when someone claimed to have discovered a process for producing cold fusion, the holy grail of sustainable energy research; or the discredited paper that tried to implicate the MMR vaccine in the development of child autism and is doing enormous damage to the uptake of childhood vaccinations, with the result that cases of measles are now on the rise again. Neither of those sets of researchers followed rigorous scientific procedures and both were soundly refuted by further study. If anyone wants references, I can give you them."*

*A few students murmur their interest.*

*"I'll put them on the module website."*

*Brigg makes a note.*

*Ben is frowning. He looks hard at Brigg.*

*"I'm not quite sure where we're going with this, John," he says in a puzzled tone. "I understand about the stimulus-response in a flatworm, but what about all the animals that have eyes like ours? We say they can form an image, but isn't that just because we can? If what we are saying about our own image being something we create in our consciousness, wouldn't that imply that those animals were conscious as well? You joked about flatworms, but wouldn't it mean that frogs and mice had consciousness?"*

*His frown has deepened whilst he was talking and there is a general murmuring of discussion around the room as some students appreciate what he is saying.*

*Brigg purses his lips. Exactly. In one remark, Ben has justified the rather self-indulgent improvisation he has embarked on this afternoon.*

*"Ah yes..." he says quietly, "I wondered if someone might pick up on that... There's definitely a conflict, isn't there?"*

*The question is gratifying, but he knows he's got to keep some kind of focus to the session. The time is limited and not everybody will be engaging at the same philosophical level as Ben. He needs to be concise.*

*"Maybe there isn't normally an image from a vertebrate eye; presumably, the image only arrives once consciousness arrives. Maybe evolution produced very sophisticated mechanisms for adapting behaviour in a stimulus-response way that only came into their own as consciousness developed. Or, maybe," he says thoughtfully, "it was the other way round – the development of sophisticated sense organs drove the development of consciousness. Maybe frogs and mice do have some kind of primitive awareness, caused by their sophisticated sensitivity. The truth is, I don't know – and I will never know what it is like to be a frog."*

*Ben is thinking hard. "This is fascinating, John; we seem to be going deeper and deeper."*

*Brigg nods. "And that's the extraordinary power of science, isn't it? The more you think you understand, the more you realise what you don't."*

*He continues, deflecting the focus of Ben's question. "But it's definitely worth making the effort to think about what we mean by sensitivity. The physical world consists of entities,*

*entities which must inevitably interact with each other. From the emergence of the very first particles, this has always been the case. As some of those interactions produced the first self-sustaining and self-replicating entities which we can start to think of as a form of proto-life, those interactions coming from the outside were of crucial importance to them, from collisions with molecules to the changes that the electro-magnetic radiation bathing the universe would make to their structures. Over aeons of time, those self-sustaining structures withstood or were changed by the buffeting they were receiving and the ones that did not withstand it simply degenerated back into the milieu. Those interactions were the beginning of what we could call sensitivity. There was radiation, there were collisions, there were all kinds of potential chemical reactions: all of them could affect structures in one way or another, some compromising their integrity, some enhancing it. But above all, those interactions contained information; information for each structure about what was outside it. It's still the same now, it's just that the structures are much more complex. Our bodies, as are those of all living things, are being bombarded with stimuli from the outside, each of which carries information. Through billions of years of reaction to those stimuli and the changes in structure that they caused, there has emerged a dizzying plethora of organisms and a wide variety of responses, from general bodily sensitivity to concentrations of response in more focused organs. There are similarities in those responses and the structures of sense organs, because we are all part of one evolving life story on this planet.*

*"If you compare that to our intuitive model of sensitivity, it's somewhat at odds. We think of ourselves as reaching out and grasping the world; this suggests it is the other way round.*

*The world comes to us. We don't see because we are looking out; we see because the outside world is reaching us. It makes us realise we are not separate; we are as immersed in the world as a buttercup or a butterfly, and it is a wonderful thing. Moreover, without the interaction of the outside on the inside, there would have been no change, no evolution at all. The way each organism, each person, processes the information will vary; none of us will react in exactly the same way. That variation is the grist to evolution's mill, and it is why we have a world of such extraordinary variety."*

*Brigg stops; he's gone on far too long. He can see there are some who look doubtful and he knows there are many points of argument in what he has just said which he cannot address today. He is in danger of confusing the session. That was what happened when you flew by the seat of your pants. He studies the students' faces. They are engaged and he knows they will respond. He collects his thoughts; can he really avoid talking about consciousness? Everything is so connected...*

It was the processing that was going wrong. To outward appearance, Marie no longer had the ability to process much of the information coming to her from her senses and little ability to respond to what she could. But was that true? The incident with breakfast and the soiled pad suggested that there was still a considerable amount of processing; that she had cognisance of her personal state. Her response had not been simply a generalised expression of discomfort; it was focused and articulate. She had been cruelly robbed of her power of speech and all its accompanying complexity of communication, but that did not necessarily mean she no longer knew something of what was happening.

Yes, there was an inexorable decline, but it was slow and painfully nuanced. Brigg had learnt to temper his urge to see a pattern in its development; if he reached such a conclusion, he was invariably wrong.

But the processing was definitely going wrong. Not because it was giving Marie an alternative perception of the world - for who can say what the correct perception is? - but because it was preventing her physical body from functioning in a self-sustaining way. The degradation of her brain was affecting not only her cognitive awareness, but also the control over those much more primitive neuro-muscular behaviours of movement and internal bodily function. That was the real sign that the body was in error mode. A living body is a point of generation, a dynamic centre where the external meets the internal, where a constant flow of energy drives a continual interchange of molecules to maintain a perpetuating, adapting presence. To understand fully that moment of becoming would be fully to understand life, and such knowledge is agonisingly closed to us; but what is certain is that any living entity is, by its very existence, inexorably linked to the very first time such a process started, if there were such a time at all. There can be no break in the chain and it makes us all, truly, billions of years old, if that is a meaningful way to measure existence. The *raison d'etre* of each moment of generation is to maintain itself by generating the next, and once it begins to lose the ability to do this, it is an indication that the process and processing are failing. It will come to us all; none of us will exceed a certain span of renewal, whatever that might be. If there have been offspring, our process already continues in another location and will, most likely, outlast our dynamic centre; if there are no offspring, then our tiny, insignificant perturbation on the almost infinite ramifications of life will flicker and cease. Our importance lies not in ourselves, except that each one of us, by existing at all, continues the improbable quest of existence to know itself. As Brigg watched Marie sleeping, her mouth slightly open but her breathing calm, he was glad for her that they had the children. She already continued beyond herself.

The innate drive of life is so strong that the recognition of our own mortality – at a visceral, immediate level - is one of the hardest states for a person to realise. We understand that others will die; we acknowledge the inevitability as we watch parents grow old or friends or loved ones succumb to terminal illness. We grieve in shock at sudden traumatic events. But when we consider ourselves, we stand apart. These events happen in a world external to us and, whilst we know in depths of our understanding that we are merely a part of that world, it always seems separate. We are always watchers on this story of life and these tragedies play out as if on a stage in front of us, forever distanced by the curtain of our individuality. Just like the theatre, those moments when the concentration is so intense that the action enfolds us in the scene and the actors' pain is our pain and their ecstasy merely a reflection of our own, are rare indeed. Occasionally, when we look at ourselves in the mirror, we may see beyond our sense of aloof indestructability and the strange unreality of the image to recognise the ravages that time has wrought on that body of ours which we intuit as an unchanging feature of our existence. Only in such moments does the process become truly meaningful to us. The flesh which was young and full is now sunken and wrinkled; the smooth bloom of youth is now crazed and blotched with broken capillaries and the creeping pigment aberrations of age. Yet we have not noticed it! Life has played a trick on us; it has let us believe we have continued as a constant entity as the world we have navigated has shifted and evolved. We have watched seasons change, hurricanes devastate the land, glaciers retreat, volcanoes erupt, forests burn, wars wreak havoc, famines reduce people to skeletons and plagues give rise to pandemics which kill millions; but we, thankfully, have been outside. It has happened 'out there', as act upon act of a play in a theatre that, until now, we had not realised we had built for ourselves. Only in such moments do we recognise our full engagement in the plot and that we are as subject to its inevitable conclusion as are the players who have provided our entertainment. Even watching Marie decline in front of him, it was still rare for the spectacle to trigger for Brigg such intimations of his own mortality; to his shame, he would find himself continually projecting to that time when she had gone, planning what he would do. When he caught himself in this act, it would trigger a bout of guilt and self-loathing and he would hear the Catholic priests of his schooldays proclaiming mankind's immersion in the morass of the sinful nature of the world. But the answer did not lie in confession: there was no sin. Marie was not separate from him; they were bound up in the same world, her weakening presence as much a feature of his existence as his own perceived continuation. To move beyond his guilt, he had to feel the reality of the unfolding narrative that constituted all there was. There was no judgement except his own and there was no future time that lay waiting for him; there was only now. Nothing lay outside it and if God were not dead, he had to play the same game as the rest of us and deliver his lines as just another actor on the stage which encompassed them all. Yes, he was mortal and so was Marie, but he understood nothing of what that meant and he knew he could not, for there was nothing to understand. The deluded cosiness of three-dimensional eternity, conjured for centuries by monstrously disingenuous theologians to keep the masses loyal and power concentrated in the Church, was an absurd fiction which they all knew had to be untrue. This game of life, this blind fumbling of existence as it generated itself in ever more complex iterations of its nature, knew not what it was, from whence it came or whither it was bound; but because it was, it had to be. It is what makes all of us: it is what we are.

David Hume blasted a hole in our common conception of causality and demolished at a stroke our intuitive sense of an ordered, predictable space within which things progressed with determination and purpose, when he showed that cause and effect were human constructions which we place upon experience. We do not see causality; we merely observe a juxtaposition in time of one event after another. It was a ground-breaking, disconcerting insight that profoundly affected the course of philosophy and which was quickly ignored by both the Church and the public at large. We do not like such counter-intuitive ideas; they upset our sense of security. The result of Hume's idea being ignored has been that we still live within a secure and comfortable medieval world-view dominated by a fourth dimensional time-line stretching from Eden to Judgement, replete with its sense of journey. Journeys are full of cause and effect. But we are not on a journey; we are not 'going' anywhere. It may feel that we are, but that is because we believe the metaphor rather than the reality. What we are engaged in, is a project of becoming. Nothing exists before the next moment; there is no landscape through which we are travelling, with deeds to do and goals to reach.

But so powerful is the metaphor and so amenable is it to our intuition, that we all feel it at a level that dictates our responses to most experiences of our lives. When Brigg looked at his own life in the context of the current situation with Marie, he found the idea that it had all been a preparation for this time very tempting. He would muse that never had he needed his ability to be content with his own company quite so much. At times, such a tendency towards self-imposed isolation had been less than optimal in building the best relations with friends, neighbours and colleagues, particularly when he was young. But now it was not only desirable, it was essential. If he had been the kind of person who needed social interaction for equanimity of mental health, the isolation he had now would, most likely, be intolerable. So, quite possibly, would be the frugality which quasi-house-arrest placed upon him. But truly, he did not mind; as long as he could still see Cruachan from the living room and smell the seaweed in the loch when he opened the door, he was content, and he knew that, if he were forced, he could do without those as well. He did not feel the need for any more belongings and anyway, without the companionship of Marie, the thought of shopping was empty. The weekly supermarket delivery satisfied all his needs.

By lunchtime, Marie was a different person. She lay quietly, watching the television. When Brigg saw her like that, he wondered what she was thinking; what amount of the content of the programme she was understanding, or even hearing. She was so calm, it was as if she was in a trance. But she responded to him with child-like enthusiasm when he entered the room carrying the tray with her lunch, her eyes lighting in anticipation. The contrast with earlier could not have been greater.

"Lunch," he said, smiling.

"Ha!" she replied, in true conversational interchange.

Brigg raised her bed with the control pad and brought her into a much more upright position for eating. She ate well, finishing all that he had brought, including a small bowlful of apricots which he had started adding to her diet to maintain her fibre intake.

"When I've had mine, would you like to get up this afternoon?"

He half expected the common dismissive stare, but there was something about her mood that suggested today might be different. Whilst he ate his lunch, the carers arrived for their lunchtime visit and pad change; when they departed, they had about four hours to themselves. With a fresh pad, he hoped Marie would remain comfortable for the afternoon.

He tidied away the lunch dishes and decided not to ask her again, but simply to take the wheelchair straight to the bedroom. When he entered with it, she immediately got excited and started to try to roll towards his side of the bed. Her wish was obvious. Brigg was glad; she hadn't been out of bed for nearly two weeks and the prospect of a walk down the lane, or maybe even a drive in the car, was stimulating. For just a moment, the invisible walls would recede.

Much to the occupational therapist's disapproval, Brigg lifted Marie in and out of the bed – a fairly simple operation making use of the bed's ability to bring her to a sitting position. From that, he would slide her legs over the side, loop his arms under her armpits and round her back, then, carefully protecting his own back, swing her up, round and into the waiting chair. The reverse operation was slightly more difficult: because the chair was lower than the bed, it relied more on his ability to squat. Marie always protested, but, given that the alternative was sacrifice to the jaws of the praying mantis hoist, they had little option.

Once up and in the chair, it was not unusual for Marie's mood to change again, scuppering Brigg's own excitement at a trip beyond the confines of the house and garden. Sometimes, they would simply move through to the living room for a little while, where Marie would watch the television whilst he took the opportunity to wash her hair with a pre-prepared massage cap. The results were wholly inadequate, but better than nothing. At other times, he might persuade her to let him take her into the front garden, where they could walk down the path towards the lane to take in the view and breathe in the fresh air and the salty tang of the loch. But today, she was showing no such reticence. She did not demur as Brigg put thick socks on her feet and helped her into her coat; indeed, she seemed impatient for him to finish. Brigg zipped up the front and tucked a thick blanket around her legs; beneath it, she was still only in her nightie. Slipping on his own jacket, he pushed her to the door. A cry of a herring gull met them as they made their way outside. He had been wrong about the tide. Rather than ebbing, it was clearly on the rise, for the *Ascophyllum* was now rising vertically in the water, with just the tops of the long strands floating in orange-brown mats on the surface. Down amongst the forest of thick stipes, the myriad animals had resumed their lives, playing out their own everyday struggle for existence in the ceaseless rhythm of their changing environment. Sometimes, Brigg would lose himself in their world, projecting himself into their alien timeframes and immersing himself in the pulse that held the disparate elements in a unity of relevance. They were moments when his consciousness expanded beyond its usual boundaries and he felt the absurdity of individual separation.

But not today. Marie was impatient. He pushed her down the path to the lane.

"Walk? Or would you like to go for a drive?"

She was definitely indicating the car.

"A drive?" Brigg repeated; he had got it wrong so many times.

"Errss!"

It was as near to 'Yes' as it could be. Without further ado, Brigg went over to the car and installed Marie's chair in the back, desperately trying to think of where to go. He knew that once she was in the car, she'd want to move quickly.

If he had been by himself, he would have chosen to go inland, following the shore of Loch Etive through the settlements along its edge towards Bonawe, taking in the splendid views of Cruachan as it reared up to its pointed, rocky heights. After a few winding miles, he would have turned north up the narrow road that cut through to the southern shore of Loch Creran through the lonely Gleann Salach. This road, although it had the status of a B road, was little different from the unclassified lanes elsewhere. Wild and open for the first two miles, it was heavily forested with dense stands of conifers along its northern reach. Brigg did not share the fashionable distaste of conifer plantations. He recognised their usefulness to the economy and there were few places that could induce the feeling of total quiet and solitude as immersion in their dark, atmospheric depths. Granted, they were not as species-rich as the more open environment of native pine forest and, indeed, the heavy monoculture suppressed any regeneration of indigenous flora, except along the margins. But, in their emotional responses, people confused sentiment with cause. These forests were not the cause of the decline of native Scots pine forest; they had been depleted many years before: for building, for industry and for sheep. People complained that the regimented lines of trees marched up the pristine slopes of their beloved views, spoiling their enjoyment. But the land should have been forested everywhere; the wild, open hills so emblematic of the Highlands were in themselves a human construction. Forests had been felled, people cleared from their ancestral lands and sheep installed where once there had been pine, birch, heather, bilberry and a diverse ecosystem that had developed and survived since the retreat of the ice ten thousand years before. The Forestry Commission had been established after the Second World War to try to replenish Britain's severely depleted stocks of timber and now, although commercial forest had spread through the Highlands and other upland areas, it still covered only a relatively small area. We were never going to get back the ancient cover of pine, birch, alder and rowan; where we could, we would try to re-establish a little, but the damage had been done. We had forests of a different kind now, forests that were a quick way of sequestering carbon, and, no matter how inferior they might be to what had been before, they brought something to the landscape - and for that, Brigg was grateful.

That was where he would have gone, had he been by himself. On reaching Loch Creran, he would have turned west along the main road round the coast of Benderloch back to the Connel bridge; that marvel of steel engineering cantilevered out across the mouth of Loch Etive, with a span second only to the Forth bridge when it was built. Stretching across the notorious Falls of Lora, it originally carried the railway north of Oban along the shores of Loch Linnhe towards Ballachulish, and Brigg wished he could have experienced those pre-Beeching days of such peaceful, scenic travel through the West Highlands. But the railway had succumbed over half a century ago and all that was left were embankments, cuttings and these rare survivals of early twentieth century engineering.

But he knew Marie would not have liked such a route. It was winding and bumpy, and it was a long drive. After the experience of the car-sickness, he would not risk it again. No, the only way to go was to follow their minor road west to the bridge and then across to Dunbeg; a journey of only about three miles. From Dunbeg, he would turn up the short road towards Dunstaffnage and the castle. He knew there was a car park there where they could a least sit and watch the busy comings and goings of boats into the marina and the entertainment of the ever-present sea birds.

There were a few cars in the car park when they arrived, with the likelihood of more to come during the afternoon; the castle was always an attraction for tourists. The promise of good weather had held and now the sunlight was glinting on the gentle waves that ran across the water of Dunstaffnage bay. There was activity around the marina, with yachts making the most of a midday high tide. He never failed to enjoy the sight of boats. He wound down his window. As well as the low chatter of human voices around them, the air was filled with the unmistakeable sound of herring gulls, calling incessantly. They had lives of such ever-present society. He glanced in the rear-view mirror; Marie was gazing distractedly out of a side window, seemingly lost in the view. Brigg let the sounds wash over him, relaxing in the security of their inevitability. Somewhere distant, on the main road towards Oban, he fancied he could hear a siren. A group of swans was close in to the shore near the car; they gleamed white in the sun.

A few buildings stood close to the car park. To their right, there was the modern building of the Scottish Association for Marine Science research station and, close by, was the Ocean Explorer Centre; a hands-on education and entertainment venue, much loved by tourist families and their children when it rained. At the other end of the car park, the road continued towards the castle, but visitors needed to complete those last few hundred yards on foot.

They sat quietly for a little while, both lost in their own worlds. The swans moved sedately across the calm water close to the shore, their serene progress over the surface giving no indication of the means of their propulsion. Slow and gentle paddling was enough to maintain an even forward motion in these conditions. Brigg marvelled at the whiteness of their plumage. He knew little of swan society – a group of un-paired males perhaps? They continued their steady progress towards the Marine Science station and disappeared behind the trees lining the edge of the bay.

Behind them, the promontory on which the castle was built was gently wooded. From where they were parked, they looked inwards towards the crowded hills of the mainland, but behind them, less than four hundred yards away, the vista was completely different. From there, one looked out across the bright expanse of the Firth of Lorn past the island of Lismore to the enticing sight of Mull on the horizon. The island was dominated by the cone of Ben More rising just south of east, from which one's gaze was drawn to the ever-widening gap between the land to the south west and the prospect of open ocean beyond. It was the kind of view which Brigg never tired of; always changing, sometimes dark and foreboding as storm clouds drew in from the west, at others sparkling with such an intensity of light that it almost hurt the eyes. At all times, the contrast between the two sides of the isthmus was profound.

This setting was why the area was so rich in history. The bay of Dunstaffnage was, today, used mainly as a site for the marina and a safe anchorage for yachts navigating the southern Hebrides. In the past, however, it had been of much more significance: its location was of strategic military advantage. This arose not only from the sheltered harbour, but also because the rocky knoll on which the castle was built commanded views over both the inner mainland route north of Oban, where any travel through the land was forced to follow the coastline, and the outer approaches to the maritime thoroughfare of the Firth of Lorn and Loch Linnhe, penetrating some twenty miles towards the mouth of the Great Glen. The castle itself dated from the thirteenth century; the seat of the MacDougalls of Lorn. Its history was chequered. Taken by Robert the Bruce in 1308, it eventually passed to the Campbells through marriage and was garrisoned by Cromwell in 1652. Later in the century it was burnt in more conflict, then rebuilt in the early eighteenth century, until a further fire a hundred years later. Flora MacDonald was held there briefly on her route to London, after being arrested for helping Bonny Prince Charlie escape to Skye as he fled from the rout of Culloden. It is an imposing sight and a fine example of medieval castle-building. But that did not comprise the totality of the area's historical importance. Pre-dating the medieval castle, with origins that stretched back into the mists of prehistory, the fort of Dunbeg had been established at the head of the bay. According to tradition, this fort had become a seat of the ancient kings of Dalriada when they had eventually moved from their original foothold at Dunadd, further south near the narrows of Crinan. When they arrived, legend had it that they had brought the fabled Stone of Destiny with them, on which were crowned all kings of their new territory of Scotland. Now more commonly known as the Stone of Scone, the Stone of Destiny supposedly came to the nascent Scotland from Ireland, where it had gained its Gaelic name of Lia Fail and on which Irish kings had also been crowned. But the legend did not stop there. Such is the myth-building of people searching for a history and a validation, that the origins of this large, unforgiving rock of sandstone were allegedly to be found in the pages of the Bible; for was it not the same stone that Jacob had once used as a pillow? Such fanciful notions can be found in the myths of all peoples, but perhaps not all magical artefacts have such implications for transport, weighing in, as it does, at some one hundred and fifty kilograms. Eventually, perhaps because Viking raids up and down the west coast were making it more vulnerable, it was moved again in the ninth century to Scone. There, it is believed, it lay for over four hundred years until Edward Longshanks, the 'Hammer of the Scots', removed it to London and installed it in Westminster Abbey, to consolidate his power over the Scottish throne. To subdue a people completely, you exert control over their most sacred, magical sources: the symbolism of Longshanks' action was clear to everyone. But its story was still not quite finished. In 1950, four students at Glasgow university managed to steal it from the Abbey and take it back to Scotland, unfortunately breaking it into two pieces in the process. They had the stone repaired and installed it in the Abbey of Arbroath, where, in 1320, the Declaration of Arbroath had asserted Scottish nationhood and Robert the Bruce as King. It was taken back to England for another forty years, but was eventually officially returned to Scotland in 1996, where it now sits in Edinburgh Castle. However, such is the mythology surrounding the stone and the longevity of its legendary role in the sanctification of a Scottish monarch, it is still taken back to London for a coronation, to symbolise the inclusive nature of the union of the United Kingdom.

Brigg found such stories fascinating and amusing trinkets of historical interest, but laughable in their puerile suspension of mature rationality. Indeed, he longed for the day when the country he lived in might grow up and move on from the anachronism of a monarchy. To his mind, the sooner they abolished it and installed a non-executive president, the better. Granted, in constitutional power the British monarch was very much like a non-executive president, simply wheeled out on state occasions to give a focus to pomp and ceremony. But it was so much more. The Crown sat at the top of a pyramid of aristocratic wealth and privilege, maintaining a sense of class and entitlement within British society. It fostered the idea that deference was due not because of personal qualities or achievement, but because of accident of birth. It merely exacerbated division. Brigg was not naive enough to think that abolition would solve the country's social problems at a stroke; he could see the mess other nations were making even though they were republics. However, many of those had gone down the route of electing an executive president, taking the absurd step of concentrating supreme power in the hands of one person. That was a far worse solution than the British crown. The British system merely preserved an archaic social structure; the installation of an executive president had the result of legitimising enormous constitutional power in individuals, with no recognition of the frailties of human nature which would inevitably affect the result. Far from reducing the sense of entitlement that he so despised in British society, republics with executive presidents could promote it, unless the incumbents of public office were such profoundly moral people that they could put service before personal ambition. Such entitlement led in the worst cases to rigged elections, or the ranting of deposed presidents that either the electorate was wrong or that they had been illegally removed from office. Brigg longed for a mature society in which rationality and fairness ruled, but he knew with sadness that humans were too riddled with competing behavioural instincts from their evolutionary past for that to happen. However, to enshrine in one's national identity an anachronistic system that actually preserved a structure of privilege within it was offensive to him. There had to be better ways of organising society than that.

A rather fine ten metre yacht was making its way out of the marina and picking its route through the moored boats in the bay. It looked strong and sturdy; the kind of vessel one would need for sailing the complex and unpredictable waters of the Hebrides. Brigg watched its progress enviously; soon it would be gone through the gap between the castle promontory and Eilean Mor, sailing who knows where? He felt an ache for change, for new horizons. He looked in the rear view mirror again. Marie was still gazing calmly out at the loch. He took his chance.

"Shall we have a walk?"

He watched her response carefully. There was none.

"Marie," he said, a little louder, repeating it twice more.

"Marie; Marie."

She turned her head away from the window and looked at him, as if searching for the source of the sound. He stretched round in his chair and smiled at her, gaining eye contact.

"Shall we have a walk?" he repeated.

There was an expression of almost child-like innocence on Marie's face. Her eyes widened and he saw a slight smile of understanding play at her mouth.

"Shall we?" he said enthusiastically, unbuckling his seat belt and moving as if to get out.

Marie moved in her chair, suddenly impatient.

"Yess..." she said clearly.

Brigg needed no more validation. He opened up the back of the car, laid out the ramp and unclipped the wheelchair, gently pulling it down onto the tarmac of the car park. The air was sweet and fresh, and the sounds from the bay and the gulls so much clearer now they were outside. As Brigg breathed deeply, drinking in the joy of being out and away from the cottage, he could see Marie also looking excitedly around her. He quickly locked the car and pushed her across the car park to the road that led towards the castle. This road ran in an arc round the last three hundred metres of the bay, terminating in a small parking area from which an offshore pontoon was accessible via a wide ramp that adapted to the state of the tide. The ramp was barred by high metal gates, preventing unauthorised access to the pontoon. About a hundred metres before it, a path branched off and climbed gently to the castle. Except for the grounds surrounding the castle, the whole promontory was lightly wooded with a delightful range of deciduous trees. It was a very pleasant scene.

Marie's chair was well-constructed and lightweight; pushing it up the slope to the castle was not arduous for Brigg. They had negotiated far more taxing gradients than that in their time. Getting into the castle, however, was a more impossible task; access was up a flight of stone steps. It did not matter. Even when she was still mobile and could manage, with difficulty, such an obstacle, Marie was not much interested in this kind of historical monument. She would remark that they all looked rather similar and was content merely to view them from outside. Brigg had to admit she was right, but he was always drawn to explore, seeking the detachment from the everyday that immersion in the atmosphere of the ruins would bring. Today, however, there was no question of that option.

The path curved round the south side of the castle, where the largely intact curtain wall stood defiantly on an impressive outcrop of rock. It was a fine sight, but Marie seemed to be paying little attention to it. Her head was bowed and her gaze seemed to be fixed on the grass a few metres ahead. Brigg wondered if it was lack of interest, or just that her muscle tone had become so weak that she could no longer hold her head straight. There were a few tourists on the path; mostly, they smiled at them, moving off the hard surface to allow them to pass. They walked to the head of this path, where a track continued to a rocky inlet a little way down through the trees, then retraced their steps to where another path led off to a ruined chapel a little way further on. This was a level track, with a firm surface, if a little rough.

"Shall we go down to the chapel?"

Marie didn't respond. Brigg turned the chair towards the path. Very often, it was the physical stimulus that would get the reaction, if there were to be any at all. Marie did not object.

"Let's go down," said Brigg. "It's a nice afternoon and the woods will be very pretty."

He was right about the woods. Every now and then the sun would break through the high clouds and shafts of light streamed through the loose stands of ash, birch and oak, falling on the understorey of bramble, grasses, ferns and moss. It could lift the most tired of spirits. This was what the objectors to coniferous plantations wanted and of course they were right in their sentiment. There was always a joy to be found amongst the open, wooded hills of the Highlands, where the light would play on the delicate leaves of the trees and the lichen encrusted bark of their trunks. There were few places in all the world that Brigg would rather be on a fine late spring morning than a thousand feet up on a hillside, in one of the few remaining examples of the ancient Caledonian forest. These woods were hardly of that quality, being mostly deciduous planting for aesthetic amenity, but, as the sun shone through, they still produced an upsurge of well-being in him. He hoped Marie was feeling something of it as well.

What was she feeling? He ached to have contact with her, to share in a mutual joy from the stimulus, as they had done on so many occasions. From his vantage point behind the wheelchair however, she still appeared to be leaning forward, her head a little bowed.

"Beautiful trees," he said, hoping to elicit some kind of response. There was none that he could make out from where he was. He stopped the chair and went round to look at Marie. She seemed to be staring slightly to one side, into the trees, a calm expression on her face.

"The trees are lovely, aren't they?" he repeated quietly, not wishing to disturb her reverie.

He thought he saw a flicker of a smile play round her lips. He followed her gaze, but could see nothing different in that particular area of the woodland.

It was one of the hardest aspects of her condition. He could still communicate with her, about things like the menu for lunch or whether she was going to get up, but conversation had gone. Her mind was now a closed book. He could tell if she was content – he could not use the term happy with any certainty – or if she was agitated or in discomfort, but he had no way of knowing what, or whether, she was thinking. Of course, none of us know what it is like to be someone else, but in normal social intercourse we receive clues about the mental states of our companions through conversation and innumerable physical gestures or facial expressions. Such elements had dwindled away almost to nothing with Marie. The moments of communication had become more and more infrequent, until the brief glimmers had finally guttered and gone out. Marie had stopped trying. Whether that had been through frustration or because the changes in her mental state had made it no longer of importance, he could not say; it was probably a mixture of both. Her inner life was now closed and the deep, subliminal sense of companionship that had been an unspoken bedrock of their married life had faded away. He had lost his Marie. But it was a bereavement for which he was unable to grieve, for she had not died. She was still a real physical presence that he had to care for and somewhere inside her there was still a mental life that he had to respect. The woman who lay in the bed all day was still Marie, she was in Marie's body, and that body was still the repository of Marie's experiences, experiences that were now locked away from him forever. He was bereaved a dozen times each day. It was cruel and Brigg felt the anguish keenly. He was desperate to grieve, but left only with tension that had no outlet. All he could do was suppress it, forcing it from his mind, immersing himself in immediacy and the intensity of the present. If he dwelt on the maelstrom of emotions that wanted to rise to the surface of his consciousness, he knew he would succumb to self-pity. He knew he would wish it to end, but that only meant one thing. At those times, the reality of his situation could fill him with despair.

Only once, recently, had he been granted a glimpse of her inner life. It had been a moment out of nowhere, a sudden flowering of memory of such intensity that the tears had flowed down her cheeks and she had held to him for reassurance and comfort. For just a few minutes, the deep bond of common experience and connection had been re-established. She had been lying in her usual state of outward detachment, watching the television. A familiar series in which expert craftspeople mended various broken artefacts was playing. It was nearing the end. Brigg was in the kitchen, starting to organise the evening meal. He could hear Marie making low noises, interspersed by the occasional exclamation. After a little while, however, he became aware that her expressions had changed; they seemed much more intense and rhythmical. She was sobbing. He stopped what he was doing and hurried to her room. She was staring at the television, one arm reaching out towards it. As he came in, she turned to him, a desperate, beseeching look in her eyes. He moved across to her and took her hand, glancing at the television. Marie grasped his hand fiercely, her sobs bursting into heaving wails of anguish. Brigg knew instantly what was happening. The ceramics expert on the programme had just mended a small plate and was handing it back to the owner, a woman. It contained a memento of the participant's mother, in the form of a sepia portrait. The woman was crying, overcome with emotion at having the precious memory of her mother restored. The programme capitalised on such moments, one could say they almost contrived them. They certainly exploited them when they happened; they were good for audience involvement. As the woman on the television wiped away her tears, Marie clung to Brigg's hand, staring up at him, filled with the sweet pain of a memory of her own. Her mother had died when she was young, and Brigg had never met her. But all through their life together, Marie had kept alive her memory, with such commitment that this person he had never met had become a central part of the narrative of his own life. Marie had kept a special photograph, taken when her mother was in her early twenties. This, too, was in sepia. Even to someone who had not met her, it was obvious that she had been striking. The sight of the sepia portrait on the plate had been the stimulus to open perhaps the most powerful memory that Marie held deep in her psyche. She was seeing her mother after all these years. Brigg held her hot, wet and shaking hand, gently stroking the back, letting her sob deeply as joy and grief passed through her in equal measure. "I know," he said quietly; "your mum." She stared at him with a yearning and a connection that he had not had for a very long time. "She was beautiful," he said, still stroking gently. Slowly, the convulsions lessened and Marie withdrew again into her own space. Brigg let go of her hand. He pulled the duvet back to let her cool; her nightie was soaked in sweat. He would ask the carers to change it before she settled for the night. Marie's eyes dimmed again and he stepped back. "I'll go and get your tea," he said. She did not look at him; the link had broken again. But it had been there, and it had been powerful. He went back to the kitchen to assuage his grief in cooking.

The chapel dated from the about the same time as the castle and lay in a simple rectangular ruin. Much archaeological excavation had been carried out on both the castle and the chapel in the twentieth century and the remaining walls were in good repair, showing some quite intricate ornamentation around the windows. They walked round both the outside and inside, before Brigg rejoined the path back to the castle. Marie was still calm and she appeared to be looking around. She became animated as a young couple pushing a small child of about eighteen months to two years came up the track towards them. Brigg smiled at the parents, whilst the child, a girl, giggled in her pushchair. Marie suddenly exclaimed "Lovely!" The parents, fortunately, had the good sense both to appreciate Marie's situation and not to appear surprised at such an unusual outburst. They laughed with her and let her engage with their toddler. Brigg stopped momentarily and stepped round the wheelchair slightly to see Marie's face. She was beaming at the child, who was in that delightful stage that babies inhabit as they turn from being helpless infants to active beings engaged on their first exciting forays into conscious exploration of the world. Marie was enraptured. The encounter only lasted a few moments, with the parents saying 'bye byes' for their child and moving on towards the chapel, with no realisation of how significant their presence on the path had been. He pushed Marie back through the woods towards the open clearing where the castle stood, feeling again a sense of warmth and connection. Looking at Marie's slightly bowed head from behind and above, he could hear her talking softly to herself as they moved through the trees. There was something about the manner in which she held herself that convinced him she was smiling. As they broke out of the woods into a burst of sunshine across the short green grass, Brigg could not suppress the tears. Love was an emotion that he found hard to understand, but at that moment, he did.

He pushed Marie back down the hill. When they reached the bottom, instead of returning directly to the car park, he decided to take the narrow road onward to where it terminated in a concrete jetty and a small car park. It was deserted. The jetty was not wide, but the remnants of a railway track ran across it; just a few metres of industrial archaeology that had not been removed. Instead it was left hanging in a strange void outside of time; no longer of any purpose but redolent with the clang and clatter of trucks and the shouts of workers as they loaded who knew what onto old steamers. Its very existence held a strong poignancy. It had no terminus; instead, the rails hung truncated at the end of the concrete, their invisible cargoes passing beyond on ghostly tracks as they continued their journeys into the past. Now, the rails went nowhere; their purpose amputated. To their side, ignominiously cutting one rail before it even reached the perilous uncertainty of the sheer edge of the jetty, a massive construction of steep girders framed a wide gently sloping ramp which led to the floating pontoon. A pair of large gates about two thirds of the way down barred the way. This was the thoroughfare now and the severed rails could only lie in mute resignation to their rusting demise.

They stopped on the jetty, near enough for him to see onto the pontoon and down into the clear water of the bay, but far enough away from the edge for Marie to feel comfortable. He watched her reaction keenly. There had been sufficient experiences of the sea and boats over the course of their married life for Brigg to know that Marie viewed them both with suspicion. Although she could swim and had enjoyed some experiences with the children in the local swimming baths, she would not go into the sea any deeper than her ankles, even in the early times when she could manage to walk without crutches. Her disability generated an imperative to maintain physical control over her mobility at all times and the wide, unpredictable, untameable expanse of sea unnerved her. She could not see what she was walking on. Her toes were useless and her balance poor. At any moment she might stumble on a rock or be lifted from the bottom by an incoming wave. As her condition had progressed and she had become dependent on either crutches for walking or his arm for support, the water had become a no-go area. Brigg had played with the children by himself when they had gone to the beach.

That was not to say that she did not like the sea; she just liked to view it from a secure base. Secure, as Brigg now knew very well, meant at least one metre away from any edge, such as that on the jetty or, more comfortably, two. This wariness of the sea applied to boats as well. She was fine on a boat in calm water where she could see the shoreline and she would even enjoy the different perspective that it would bring. However, once a boat, particularly a small boat, turned into the open sea, it was a different matter. Not only was the lack of a secure reference point on the land disconcerting for her, any rocking from even the slightest wave would make her feel sick. She was a very poor sailor. It was the same problem that had transferred itself to car travel. She may have had a natural tendency to motion-sickness, many people did; but it was almost certainly exacerbated by her physical condition. Even on the largest car ferries she would never sit on the open deck, choosing to remain in the relative security of the lounge, despite Brigg suggesting that it might help with her mounting queasiness. He had been left to walk the decks alone. He loved to do that; for him, there was something about boats that was indefinably exciting; they spoke of freedom and escape, whether it was the escape from the shore of his childhood when he and his brothers would go to the local boating lake, or the promise of adventure and distant lands that could, in his adulthood, be evoked simply by gazing at the bow of a ship, be it ferry, liner or container leviathan.

He gazed at the attractive scene of moored boats for a few minutes, expecting Marie to indicate an impatience to be moving. She did not. Her head was still a little bowed and she may have been looking at the edge of the jetty, yet it was just as possible that her attention was further afield, or nowhere.

He wondered why she was so calm this afternoon. There seemed no pattern to her slow decline, except that it was, inexorably, just that. It still had the power to surprise, and this afternoon was one of those times. There was a boat moored at the pontoon and he wished he could go down and look at it more closely, but the gates were shut. Besides, there were various signs on the girders framing the entrance to the ramp, making it clear that unauthorised access was discouraged. He knew the boat to be the RV Calanus, a research vessel used by the Scottish Association for Marine Science. Brigg liked the name. Rather than choosing one of the great icons of the western seas, like a dolphin, a killer whale or a basking shark, they had decided to immortalise a humble copepod, a member of the plankton and one of the smallest animals to be found in the sea. Indeed, most people probably did not even know of their existence; you could only see them down a microscope. But they were common, and, along with all planktonic species, hugely important in the grand picture of ocean – and thus global - ecology. Different species of *Calanus* could be used as markers for the varying bodies of water that made contact with British shores. Brigg remembered the hours he had spent in his marine studies identifying the plethora of species in different plankton samples. Certain species would come and go, but always there were copepods, and water from the south-western approaches would be replete with the majestic *Calanus finmarchicus*, its long antennae outstretched to hold its body in the water column. He had enjoyed those times. Now, as he looked at the sturdy, blue-painted vessel lying quietly at its mooring, he felt an urge to go closer. It was tantalising. The tide was high and the ramp sloped very gently; it would have been perfectly safe to push the wheelchair down. However, he could understand: there was obviously still a commercial purpose to the mooring, albeit much reduced from earlier times when the railway had brought or taken whatever cargo the boats had carried. He fancied it might have been herring, a local reflection of the more major developments at Mallaig and Ullapool. Today the pontoon was quiet, but of course it was important that safety was maintained.

Brigg looked wistfully at the bay and the moored boats for a few more moments. The hulls shone white, bringing cheer to the grey of the water, the masts of the marina casting silver accents against the deep green of the hillside beyond. To the left, Cruachan's top was once again shrouded in cloud; a harbinger of more weather approaching. Just over a low headland, he could see the top of the steel framework of the Connel bridge, a reminder of their new home and the long finger of Loch Etive probing deep into the hills, taking his imagination on another impossible journey away from the bounded nature of his current circumstances. Marie began to move impatiently in the chair; it was time to go. Reluctantly, he turned away to retrace their steps across the jetty and onto the road back to the car park.

Brigg had got as close to the edge as was possible, whilst maintaining Marie's sense of security, enabling a good view for both of them of the boats and the water. In order to do this, he had positioned Marie's chair across the rails as they led to the end of the jetty and the entrance to the ramp. He had manoeuvred the front castors of the chair carefully across the inner rail and then stopped, leaving sufficient distance to the edge. Pushing a wheelchair forward over uncertain ground was always more difficult than reversing, for the castors would be prone to catching in the slightest rut, sometimes with alarming results. In the worst cases, all forward motion would be brought to an abrupt stop, jolting the occupant of the chair forward. In previous times, when Marie had still been able to get in and out of the chair to enter a shop or some other activity, neither he nor she had always been as diligent about ensuring that she was strapped into the chair as he was now. In the worst cases, if the castors had caught when they had been walking quickly, the violence of the sudden braking would not only jar the chair with startling force, but could even tip Marie out and onto the pavement, as had happened once in Brighton or, more devastatingly, onto the road, as had occurred on one memorable occasion in Edinburgh. It was this latter event that had finally consolidated Brigg's determination to make sure he had always fastened her lap belt. Marie had been tipped into the path of fortunately slow-moving oncoming traffic and the sight of her lying on the road, coupled with the intense shock of alarm that had gripped him, had galvanised whatever habit-forming response lay deep in the bowels of his psyche. Now, if she were amenable to going in the chair, she would often complain when he tried to strap her in; but he would not leave the house without ensuring she was.

Going backwards was always much safer. The large wheels gave control over the widest of gaps or the most severe of irregular pavements. Even going forwards, often the only way to negotiate difficult sections of a path was to tilt the chair back and proceed solely on the rear wheels, until smoother ground was gained. Brigg reversed the chair carefully, pulling the castors safely over the rail, intending to swing the chair so that it pointed towards the narrow road leading to the car park. He felt something catch at his right foot. The next moment, the harmony of predictability that action follows intention was shattered. He was falling. Absurdly, he found himself lying sideways on the ground, his legs sprawled, the right-hand wheel of the chair rolling over his ankle. As he had fallen, he had been forced to release the handles, but he had also twisted the chair onto a new trajectory. His shoulder hit the concrete. This protected his head, but all he could do was watch in a kind of suspended astonishment as the chair, freed from his control, continued its progress over his leg, powered now by nothing more than the momentum provided by a last wild flailing of his arm. This had swung it round, so that the other rear wheel followed its opposite number and also began to progress towards the ramp. He lay helplessly, watching the chair straighten itself enough to roll onto the gently sloping surface, catching a glimpse of Marie's face as she stared with wide-eyed surprise at the unfamiliar environment of girders and link fencing. Then she was gone, out of his sight, rolling slowly down the smooth surface, gradually picking up speed.

He had tripped on the lip of the ramp. Where the ramp articulated with the jetty, there was one area where friction from daily use had produced enough erosion of the concrete to produce a slight gap. Concentrating on the front castors of the chair, he had not been looking at where he was placing his feet and had caught his heel where the metal edge of the ramp had been exposed. This had sent enough force through his ankle to undermine his normal ability to maintain balance. Stability had been replaced by random motion. So unaware is our conscious mind of the myriad adjustments our body engages in every moment as we stand or move in the world, that we only recognise them by their absence. It is only when the unintentional usurps the intentional, when randomness replaces predictability, that we become aware that harmony is something that we generate and maintain from moment to moment and not a necessary state. Moreover, that recognition is not instantaneous. Our acceptance of a harmonious, ordered progression through the world is so ingrained that, even when such a disturbance occurs, the acknowledgement of the crisis is not immediate to consciousness. As Brigg had fallen backwards, the visual sense-data of the strange angle his body was making with Marie's chair and the touch-data of the passage of the wheels over his sprawling legs had arrived in the brain well before his conscious awareness had registered what had happened. It took, perhaps, only two seconds for his brain to be galvanised into a realisation that a serious event was unfolding, but by then the damage was done and the wheelchair, with Marie strapped into it, was on its way down the ramp.

His conscious mind shook itself into action as the potentially catastrophic nature of the situation burst through the fog of his bewildered awareness. The ramp was sloping and Marie had no way of slowing its acceleration. There were about ten metres of ramp before the metal gates, with another five before reaching the pontoon. Marie was already about half way down. He twisted himself, scrambling to get to his feet. The chair had brakes, which could be operated by either the attendant or the occupant herself, by pushing on two levers which would press knurled metal rods onto the tyres. But Marie was not capable of that. In the past, when she still had use of both her arms and some capacity to process action and consequence, they would try to practice the idea of emergency braking, should something catastrophic happen to him as he was pushing. He would go down a slope and ask her to take responsibility for braking the chair, keeping only the slightest control over their descent, hoping that she would be able to push strongly enough to bring the chair to a halt. She never could. She might slow its progress a little, but could never stop it. After a few attempts, Brigg was resigned to the unavoidable truth that, in reality, he was indispensable. Besides, he knew that, even had she been able to exert enough pressure on the levers, it was very unlikely that she would have processed a situation quickly enough to avert an accident. Whatever was going to unfold due to the external forces he had set in motion, would unfold.

By the time he was on his feet, there was no chance that Brigg could stop Marie's progress down the ramp. Modern wheelchairs are designed to have a minimum of friction and Marie was accelerating happily down the albeit gentle slope. As Brigg scrambled upright, he could only watch helplessly, his mind projecting at a furious rate a series of possible outcomes, all calamitous. Her feet would be trapped; she might break an ankle. He would be needing to phone for an ambulance. What if she tipped forward and hit her head? Or the castors caught on something and the chair fell to one side, perhaps trapping her arm between it and the ramp? He was moving now, catapulted into action: a desperate sprint to try to reach the chair before disaster struck.

Then he stopped, hardly believing what he was seeing. There was to be no calamity. Those of a religious disposition would have attributed it to divine intervention, a guiding hand from on high that had magically intervened. A Guardian Angel, perhaps, or the good Lord responding to all the prayers of the faithful for the sick and needy. The explanation was much more prosaic, yet no less miraculous for Brigg, if by a miracle one means an insertion into an event another, which for the observer is impossible to predict. In truth, of course, there was no miracle. What happened was wholly predictable; it was just impossible for Brigg to foresee. Although the instigator of the random events that had set the whole sequence in motion, his sprawling involvement did not give him access to the full set of initial conditions. He watched in amazement as the chair, instead of rolling headlong down the slope towards the gates as he had imagined it would, ran in a path that made it brush against the chain link fencing lining the steel frame. At the angle it made contact, the fencing presented a smooth, slightly yielding, surface against which the left-hand rear wheel rubbed smoothly, slowing the forward motion. Fortunately, Marie had taken to holding her arms across her body, so there was no possibility that her arm might become trapped. The propelling ring of the wheel clattered against the links, with friction gradually slowing the chair's motion. It did not quite stop it, but by the time the chair reached the closed gates, all that was left of that motion was dissipated in nothing more than a gentle bump of the footrest and the tips of Marie's toes against the forgiving link covering. As Brigg had fallen, he had imparted enough force on the handle to turn the chair, but not enough to bring it all the way round to a motion parallel to the side of the ramp. Its trajectory meant that the gentle collision with the side of the ramp was inevitable, and that the chances of physical harm to Marie were very low. There was never going to be a calamity; once set in motion, the whole sequence would play out in only one way.

He stopped only for a moment, then ran down to where Marie was now resting against the gate, a new concern now gripping him that she would be in a state of shock from the trauma of the event. Her head was raised and, although he was certain she had not experienced any significant physical hurt, he expected to see anger or distress in her expression. There was neither; she was laughing.

Brigg stared at her, trying hard not to let his confusion and surprise show in his face as he quelled the outpouring of apology and explanation that he was about to deliver. He forced his mouth into a grin whilst his wide eyes and furrowed brows still conveyed the agitation that a sudden infusion of adrenaline into his system had produced. Fortunately, Marie was not looking at him, otherwise she might really have been traumatised by the extraordinary expression that resulted. Instead, she was looking through the gates towards the pontoon, where the RV Calanus lay peacefully tied to her mooring.

"Well, that was a bit different!" Brigg managed to say, overcome with relief that a disaster had been averted.

This time, Marie did turn to him. Her eyes were shining. Brigg's features relaxed a little and he smiled at her properly. Sometimes, she would laugh at something in such a manner that he knew she was being ironic and that underneath the apparent humour lay anger. Not this time. Her face was filled with pure delight; she looked truly happy.

Brigg still had the image of Marie's surprised expression as the chair had bounced over his spread-eagled legs, but as he made himself laugh with her, he realised that she had not been looking at him; the almost fixed angle of her head meant that she had been focusing down the ramp. It suddenly struck him that she might not even have registered that he had let go of the chair. After all, he was always behind it; an unchanging feature of her experience and taken for granted. He was always there, and if she was moving, it must be because he was causing it. There weren't many times when he could say her dementia was an advantage, but at that moment it truly was. He glanced down at her feet to make sure that nothing untoward had happened to them, but he knew before he looked that they were fine. She would have complained by now. The adrenaline rush was subsiding and he could feel his body start to relax. Once again that afternoon, tears pricked at his eyes, the flood of wholly incongruous emotions that were coursing through him resolving in a sudden overwhelming sensation of love for the woman who had been his constant companion for so many years.

He heard a voice behind him.

"Are you okay?"

He turned to see the father of the little girl in the pushchair standing at the top of the ramp. He was a little out of breath and had obviously been running.

"We saw you fall over," he said. "Is everything alright?"

Brigg smiled at him. The surge of relief he was feeling made him a little light-headed. He could see the woman and the toddler walking down the path towards the jetty; the man must have sprinted from a long way off. Brigg's smile broadened.

"Yes it is, thank you! I'm not quite sure what happened there; I must have tripped. Fortunately, no harm done! That was good of you to come over."

"It looked a bit worrying from where we were," the man said, his own breathing calming.

Brigg pushed Marie up the ramp towards him. She gave an exclamation of delight when she saw the woman approaching with the little girl. The sensation of good fortune can manifest in many ways and for Brigg at that moment it became so powerful that he experienced a sudden weakness in his limbs as a wave of gratitude flooded his consciousness. They had been unbelievably lucky. Moreover, how wonderful was it that this perfect stranger had run to help. He felt humbled. The man must have reacted instinctively. A deep-seated behavioural response, deriving from aeons of social interaction within our species' evolutionary past and probably reinforced by strong educational conditioning in his childhood, had driven him to rush to someone's aid. As his wife joined them, also looking concerned, Brigg again felt a welling of emotion, this time as a response to that most estranged sensation for him: an immersion in his own humanity.

The woman's concern soon lightened as she realised all was well. She smiled at them both.

"That looked serious. Were either of you hurt?"

Brigg managed to keep control of his brimming emotions. "No, we're fine, thank you." He glanced down at the edge of the ramp. "I think I must have tripped on this," he said, tapping at the exposed edge with his foot. "It was good of your husband to come running over."

The man laughed. "No problem; just glad you're both okay." He looked at Marie. "It doesn't seem to have affected your wife."

Indeed, Marie appeared oblivious to their conversation. She was instead laughing at the little girl, who was herself giggling back at her, her eyes bright with delight at Marie's attention.

It was time to go back to the car; they needed to get home before the carers were due to visit again. The young family walked along the path with them, much to both Marie's and their daughter's pleasure. The little girl seemed fascinated by Marie's chair; presumably, to her, just another sort of pushchair: one that adults used. They were local people, with soft, West Highland accents. Eilidh and Lachlan, with a little girl called Ailsa. They had come up from Oban for the day. They had assumed from Brigg's accent that they were tourists and were quite surprised to hear that they were living on Loch Etive. Conversation was so easy and so natural that, by the time they reached their cars, Brigg had explained much of how they had come to move North, including an outline of Marie's condition, although for this he spoke softly, never quite knowing how much she would understand, should she overhear. He need not have worried, for Marie was much too taken with Ailsa than to be listening to him. It was ordinary, casual, friendly interaction, but for Brigg it was ten minutes of pleasure; the first proper conversation he had held with someone other than a health professional for a long time. As they said their goodbyes at the car and he began attaching the restraining straps for the wheelchair, he was delighted when Eilidh suggested that he and Marie should come to visit them some day.

"That would be very nice," he said, searching her face for confirmation that she was not simply being perfunctory. That she was not, was transparent in the warm smile and the welcome in her eyes.

"Thank you," Brigg continued; "and you must come to us." He smiled down at Ailsa. "Perhaps we can all go down to the loch and play."

The little girl probably had no idea what he was talking about, but she giggled happily at him.

"We will," replied Eilidh. She bent down to her daughter. "It would be lovely to go and see Marie and John, wouldn't it?"

The girl giggled more, squirming in her pushchair in evident excitement. The tone of her mother's voice was conveying a joy to come.

Lachlan swapped his phone number with Brigg. "Better use WhatsApp rather than anything else," said Brigg. "The signal is a little dodgy at times, but we have Wi-Fi in the house."

With last goodbyes, he pushed Marie up the ramp into the car and secured the chair, fastening her safety belt. As he drove back to the main road, he looked in the mirror at her. She looked content and peaceful, a gentle smile making her appear more alive than she had for a long time. She looked like Marie, the Marie that he used to know.

*It is Holly who starts the discussion. Brigg had noticed that the frown on her face had grown deeper as he had been talking, as if a question is troubling her.*

*"So," she says in a puzzled tone, "you're saying that when I look at the world, I'm not really seeing it, I'm sort of making up what I think I see from certain bits of information from it. In that case, how do I know that what I'm seeing is right? You might be seeing more than me."*

*"You don't," Brigg replies. "In all probability, you see more than I do; after all, I wear glasses, don't I? And, of course, that doesn't just apply to seeing, does it? It's probably easier to envisage if you think about other senses, such as hearing, or taste. I can almost guarantee that you hear more than I do, because the sensitivity to the higher frequencies fades as you get older, and my sense of smell and taste are also fading. So*

*who's world is the right one there? And there again, any person's hearing is really only quite modest in its capacity when you compare it to a dog's."*

*He smiles at Holly, who appears to be processing the implications of this. "However, the point is, I'm glad I can pick up what I can; it's still useful to me. It stops me getting knocked down by a bus."*

*Holly purses her lips. "But if I don't see the world as it is, then presumably animals don't, either. If a mouse doesn't see a cat for what it is, it's not going to be able to escape, is it?"*

*Brigg shrugs. "Well, sometimes they don't. Maybe," he adds, "those are the ones with the slightly poorer sight, and they'll have fewer offspring, though it's probably not that simple."*

*Animated discussion breaks out around the room. Amanda turns to Holly and says:*

*"Mice see a shape, don't they, and even though it might not be a whole cat, they've learned to react to that shape. Those that don't won't survive."*

*"Or maybe they just run from any movement," someone else suggests. "That would be programmed into them from their genes. It's a very primitive survival strategy."*

*Ben chips in. "Actually, that's fascinating, because if you keep quite still, like a cat would, the mouse won't know you're there. It makes you wonder if they see the shape at all. It's completely different from birds – they react to shapes. If our cat just lies in the garden without moving, the blackbirds and robins will still go into overdrive with their alarm calls."*

*"Our cat doesn't seem to notice anything until it moves, either," says Amanda. "She seems to stare vacantly into space."*

*Holly is still frowning. "Yeah, but mice and cats have got eyes like ours, haven't they? Why can't they see the world properly?"*

*Brigg smiles. "What do you mean by properly?"*

*Holly hesitates. "Well, as it is..." she says, her voice lacking conviction as the conflict in her understanding becomes apparent to her. The frown returns. "This is very confusing, John. There's a world outside and the light from the world reaches me, or the cat, or the mouse or whatever. It goes in our eyes, which are very similar to the cat's eyes, or the mouse's. We can see the mouse, whether it's moving or not and know that there's a mouse there. What Ben and Amanda are suggesting is that the cat or the mouse don't see anything."*

*Vicky, who had been confident of her knowledge of the structure of the retina, suggests: "Their eyes are similar to ours, Hol, but they have different levels of rods and cones in them; that makes it easier or harder for them to see certain things, particularly if the light isn't right. And I don't think they see in colour like us. Besides, their brains are different from ours, they're not as complex."*

*"Yeah, but that doesn't necessarily mean their senses are worse than ours: think of what John just said about dogs' hearing."*

*Vicky reflects on this. "Well, yes, in a way, but their processing must be different, mustn't it? Otherwise, they'd see the mouse. Although, of course," she adds thoughtfully, "maybe they do still see it, but are being cunning."*

*Brigg is gratified by the level of discussion that is going on all around the room. He notices that Megan, sitting by the window, appears to be preparing to contribute. The sky is now dark and the November chill has settled over the campus.*

*Lights stud the buildings and students can be seen hurrying across the well-lit space of the concourse outside. Brigg feels a glow of acceptance and security as the warm fellowship of the room draws everyone in. This group of students have known each other for over two years and seem to have developed a strong bond.*

*He becomes aware that Megan is already speaking.*

*"It's something to do with figure-ground relationship, isn't it? I remember doing something about it in A level psychology. It's why optical illusions work; the brain has to work out what's there, it doesn't just see everything straight away. It's not until the 'figure' stands out from the 'ground' that we notice anything at all. It's how camouflage works, like a tiger's stripes. Because they blend in with the shadows of the grass stalks, you can't make out the figure of the tiger itself. When you think of it, Hol, we don't always see something like a mouse straight away, particularly if it's against a dark background. We have to work out the shapes first. Maybe our brains are just better at doing that than a cat's."*

*Holly is still uncertain. "Yes, I know that," she says, a little irritated. "I get the stuff about nerve transmission and brains – well, I sort of do – but we're all looking at the same world, aren't we? Even if our brains have to sort out what we see, there's still a cat, or a mouse, or a tiger out there, isn't there? But now we seem to be saying that there might be other things out there that I can't see. How do any of us know that what we're looking at is right?"*

*Megan purses her lips. "Well... I suppose we don't."*

*Another male student, Richard, joins in. "Yeah. We all might be seeing different things. I might see a cat, but not a mouse and you might see a deer but not a tiger. I can't know what you are seeing and you can't know what I am."*

*"Yes, but they're all there," says Holly.*

*"Well, I suppose they are," agrees Richard. "But I can only really know what I can see, can't I? Maybe none of us sees the world properly."*

*"What, you mean there are things there that we can't see or know about?"*

*"Yeah...maybe... Not that there are holes in my world or anything like that, but more that I don't know whether what I see is what you see, even if we agree we're looking at the same thing. My world may be different from yours. If the picture of my room is in my head; how do I know what picture you've got in yours?"*

*"Oh, that's silly!" says Holly exasperatedly. "You can see this room; I can see this room. The room is here. There aren't two rooms."*

*Richard does not reply. He frowns at her, thinking.*

*Brigg can feel that the tenor of discussion around the tables is changing as possible implications of Holly's questioning permeate the room.*

*"Maybe," he says quietly, "there are not two rooms; there are twenty rooms. One for each of us. Maybe each one of us sees a different room..."*

*Holly snorts. "Oh, don't be ridiculous, John; there can only be one room."*

*Brigg shrugs. "Perhaps...But whose?"*

*"Maybe no-one's," says Richard. He turns to Amanda. "When we were thinking about what we can see of Megan, it was you, Mandy, who suggested that we don't really see anything at all; that there's nothing of a person or a thing*

*actually reaching us from the outside. We create an image in our consciousness; that means it's our image, not the person herself. It's what John and Ben were talking about a minute ago. So whatever John just said about sensitivity being receiving information from the outside, in reality we construct our own world when we look at things. It must mean that my image of Megan might be different from yours. It doesn't mean that there isn't a real Megan there, but how can I know whether I am right in how I see her? The same must apply to our picture of the room, in fact, of anything."*

*Holly's face is a picture of bewildered conflict. "Oh, for heaven's sake! That means none of us can be certain anything is real! You're suggesting that I'm making up what I see."*

*"In a way, yeah. It's odd, isn't it?" says Richard thoughtfully. "It hadn't occurred to me until John did that stuff with Megan, but the implication must be that nothing that I think I am sensing has to be as it really is; I'm sort of translating stimuli into images, or sounds and so on, rather than actually having direct access to what's out there." He frowns deeply. "In a way, I suppose I could be making the world up as I go along."*

*Holly stares at him, unable to reject his reasoning but wrestling with its unsettling nature, unwilling to let go of her previous understanding and plunge into the void that cognitive dissonance produces. Brigg wonders if she will take that leap of reason, or whether she will smother it and all its disconcerting implications. He is glad for Richard's and Ben's interventions; it is easier to dismiss an idea from a lecturer or other external agent, less so when it is starting to circulate amongst one's peers. It is why social media is so powerful. Once again, he feels a vindication for the session: these moments are important. If Holly is now feeling this cognitive conflict, then it is likely that many in the room are, if it had not occurred to them before. He wants to promote intellectually curious, critical adults, not afraid to question ideas and received wisdom. Only that way will they make good teachers, able to evaluate their practice honestly and effectively. Besides, it is their birthright as human beings; they have inherited brains with the capacity to wonder at such ideas and they should be challenged to do so.*

*He lets the students talk, making a few notes as to how he might conclude the session. When he looks up again, he is astounded to see Holly looking directly at him, her expression completely changed. The frown has gone and the tension in her demeanour has disappeared. A slight smile is playing around her mouth.*

*"That's extraordinary, John; thank you. I'd never thought about it before." The smile broadens. "I think I get it now... I think I can see what you mean. Yeah... It's odd, though, isn't it? What I see isn't outside, it's inside, inside my brain, my consciousness..."*

*Brigg returns her smile. "And I can only hope it's a nice picture in there."*

*Holly looks around at her colleagues. "You're all inside me," she says, a note of triumph in her voice. "I'm constructing you all as I sit here, from nothing more than light energy. Wow..."*

*Another puzzled expression appears on Holly's face, though this time it does not seem to be accompanied by concern. She then asks a question which makes Brigg realise that the quick notes he had just made were already obsolete.*

*"So, my consciousness," asks Holly; "where is that? Am I in my brain, or am I somewhere else, just using my brain to*

*make a picture of the world for me? In which case," she adds with a real sense of wonder, "where am I?"*

When they got home, Brigg helped Marie get back into bed, making her comfortable and switching on the small television in the corner of her room. A regional programme was showing a documentary about sheep farmers on Mull. Marie stared at the screen.

"Well, that was an interesting afternoon, wasn't it?" said Brigg as he adjusted the height and angle of the bed. "How nice to meet Eilidh and Lachlan – and little Ailsa. I wonder if they do come and see us."

Marie did not respond. She was watching a dog in the process of rounding up some sheep. Brigg knew there was no point in saying any more.

"I'll make us a cup of tea and bring a biscuit," he said, wistfully. Marie gave no indication that she had even heard his words. The camera was focusing on the dog's face as it crouched low in the grass, a few metres from the flock, waiting for the shepherd's next instruction. Brigg was no longer an element of Marie's consciousness. He went to the kitchen.

The kitchen window faced away from the loch, across the wide expanse of the Moss of Achnacree, which separated the narrowing mouth of the loch from the waters of Ardmucknish Bay. Whilst he was waiting for the kettle to boil, Brigg stared absently at the browns, greens and purples of bracken, grass and heather, reflecting on the events of the afternoon. He hardly noticed the chaffinches busily engaged in their constant drive for food and social interaction, flitting in and around the scrubby rowan trees at the edge of the garden.

As with Marie; so with him. Where is that world we think we see all the time?

The encounter with Eilidh and Lachlan was still casting a warm glow. He mused on the visceral pleasure that had been produced by such a brief experience of human contact. He was sure neither Lachlan nor Eilidh would be concerning themselves with it, but for Brigg it had touched a primeval urge that had lain suppressed beneath the weight of their everyday circumstances. He would message them in a few days, but he would only do so once, unless they replied in such a manner that implied they were serious about maintaining contact. He did not expect them to; the busy world of a young family did not intersect much with his and Marie's.

The kettle was boiling. He poured the water on the teabags, half-filling Marie's mug. She did not drink much tea and, anyway, a full mug would be a liability in the bed. She had grown used to drinking cold liquids from her normal plastic beaker, but found it difficult to form a proper seal against the thicker edge of a ceramic mug. Spills were commonplace. A brown shape flew across the garden, swooping low then disappearing as quickly as it had come. It was a shape he knew, yet a shape of such intermittent occurrence that it always grasped his attention, as if it were sent from the other half of his reality to remind him that his solipsistic reverie was not the full story of his existence. Patches of open woodland lined the edge of the loch and the hawks would hunt all along the shore, favouring the richly populated gardens of the crofts, where the human inhabitants colluded with them in their search for a meal by enticing a plethora of small birds with tables full of enticing treats. Brigg knew that it was likely this female was now positioned in one of the taller trees nearer to the water, watching and waiting for its chance. Sometimes, he would train his binoculars on the bird as it perched, stock-still against the browns of bark and foliage, its cold eye piercing the background of inconsequential disturbance for that one tell-tale flutter that would galvanise the hawk into silent, deadly flight. It never ceased to thrill him.

An event. An intrusion of unpredicted objectivity into the constant unfolding of his awareness. There was no sparrowhawk, then there was, then it was gone. Was it meaningful? Was there any reason for it, save that it was part of the complex fabric that existence generated as it flowed from moment to moment? Were not all things in life just events? What about the incident on the bridge? He had catalogued it as an accident, that he had caused it by slipping and he was grateful it had not been worse, as it would have been had the circumstances been only slightly different. But they hadn't been, and Marie had hardly noticed, or so he presumed. And anyway, what did he mean by an accident? It was a label used so commonly that its disingenuousness hid its etymology. Such is the arrogance of the human species that it presumes the world exists for it alone, that the ways in which humans decide they want to live will be the ways in which the world unfolds. Any deviation is an accident, a falsehood which should have unfolded in another way. But that was an absurd perspective, taken to extreme by the insidious mythology of ignorance peddled by preachers of the fairytale of Fall and Sin. Things could be different, if Adam had not disobeyed and brought corruption upon the world. What utter nonsense. An accident isn't a disaster, because there is no such thing as an accident. Accidents are human constructions; animals do not have accidents. Things happen to animals, or animals do things. They are events, events that manifest themselves as existence generates the next moment. They may disturb the cosiness of our constructed human predictability, but that is because we base our lives on a flawed epistemology. The induction with which we continually anticipate the Now cannot give anything other than a hopeful guide to what is to come. Induction works, most of the time, because the world is largely predictable. But its conclusions are only probable. Russell's turkey constructed a happy and predictable life for itself, until it all went wrong on Christmas Eve. A different event intervened. It was not good, it was not bad. It was simply an event, no more but no less. What we call an accident is a reminder that our perception of order and predictability is a construction that we place on our existence, and that it only exists because we maintain it. It reminds us that underneath it all, there is randomness in the universe. There is no underlying harmony; the existence we call life generates that harmony so that it can itself exist – and it must do that from moment to moment, ceaselessly overcoming the tendency to chaos around it. Normality is random; we are a defiance. Our accidents are nothing more than a momentary intrusion of that randomness, reminding us of how precarious this phenomenon of life really is.

It was easy to dismiss PPA or, for that matter Marie's CMT, as accidents to her physiology or her DNA, perhaps at conception, perhaps as a result of life choices or incidents. Such thinking was smug, it imposed norms on life and DNA, insulating those of us who are fortunate enough not to suffer from such unsavoury and debilitating conditions, allowing us to relax in the gratitude of knowing that we do not have such malfunctions within our own bodies. Again, it is disingenuous, for the relief we experience masks the certainty that other events have happened to our own genetics and that life choices we made in past are inevitably influencing our present. Changes to DNA occur every time a gamete is produced. They are not accidents, they are events and, though most have little effect, they are, in total, the engine that has driven evolution. But, perhaps even more importantly from a human point of view, those norms we imagine are also pernicious, breeding discrimination and prejudice. To view changes such as PPA or CMT as accidents is not the kindest, nor the most parsimonious, nor the most accurate way of thinking about them. They are events; just as was the sparrowhawk in the garden.

The tea bags had done their job and the resulting brew was strong and dark. Brigg poured a little milk into each and reached for the biscuit container in a nearby cupboard. He took out one of Marie's favourites, a chewy sultana and oat cookie, and returned to the bedroom. The sheep had been rounded up and the farmer was talking about the forthcoming auction in Oban. Brigg smiled. Marie's eyes were closed and she was snoring gently. He put the mug on a side table and left, leaving the door ajar. After returning the biscuit to its container, he stood in the open front door with his own tea, watching the last of the afternoon light over the loch.

He had been fortunate to take Marie out that afternoon and they had been fortunate that it had been such a rich experience. As he looked out at the loch and the gentle greying of the skies as more cloud crept in on the gentle westerly breeze, Brigg savoured the enhancement that a trip away from the house had brought. He did not know it would be the last time Marie left her bed. Perhaps it was a sense of fulfilment that her encounter with little Ailsa had brought; perhaps something about the short journey in the car had brought back memories of that ill-fated sightseeing tour when she had been so car-sick; perhaps, quite simply, a tiredness with the daily struggle of maintaining herself in the world was creeping through her body. He would not know, and neither, of course, did Marie. But she did not leave her bed again. On reflection, it wasn't a surprise, for she had been spending much longer between forays outside, but she had still occasionally got into her chair, so that she could go into their living room or sit outside on a fine day. After returning to bed that afternoon, however, it had all ceased. It was as if a switch had been thrown in her brain and so emphatic was the resulting unwillingness to move that only once did Brigg try again to coax her into the wheelchair. It had been a disaster. He had gone through their tried and tested procedures of raising the bed, swinging her legs over the side and lifting her into the waiting chair, but it had produced something akin to a panic attack. So instant and so strong had been Marie's distress, that he had immediately put her straight back in the bed, cursing himself for his insensitivity. For a period of about half an hour, it had caused her to display a bout of agitated aggression towards him, which only abated when he had left the room and she had eventually fallen asleep, the wildness in her eyes and her twisted snarls finally subsiding into deep open-mouthed snoring. As he looked at her slowly recovering flushed face and neck and the beads of sweat still visible on her forehead, he knew he would not try again, unless there were to be an emergency.

Brigg felt the familiar pricking at the skin of his face as the first of the season's midges settled down for a quick meal of his blood. Years of acquaintance with the Highlands had produced an acceptance of their presence; it was as if one had to pay for one's experience of the beauty. Another microscopic creature of equivalent size to a *Calanus*, one midge by itself was utterly inconsequential. One hardly knew it was there. But there was never one midge. They existed in populations of countless billions, covering the western seaboard from Galloway to Sutherland and filling the Highland glens with vaporous mists of invisible biomass. From late May to September, they drove the deer to the higher ground and the human inhabitants indoors, then disappeared as quickly as they had arisen. He took the last of his tea back inside the cottage. He remembered how, on that first visit to the Highlands, their naive English family from the South had tried, on their first evening, to have a game with a ball in the garden of the cottage where they had been staying. The game had, perhaps, lasted fifteen minutes before the midges had become intolerable and they had been sent scurrying back inside. Quite ignorant of such a display of nature in the raw, he had gazed in astonishment at the darkening of the window panes as the tiny creatures crowded to the light inside. By the end of the holiday they were much more experienced, and much wiser about their exposure. Not that *Culicoides impunctatus* could be avoided altogether; they were, quite emphatically, a price one had to pay for the privilege of immersion during the summer months in the unsurpassed beauty of the Highlands. Long exposure would make one more resigned to and even more tolerant of their bites, but even the few who were truly impervious to the effects could not escape the creeping itchiness that the physical sensation of thousands of microscopic insects on one's skin would cause. If possible, one had to join the deer and make for the higher altitudes: only above two thousand feet would the swarms finally thin out and be blown away by the fresh breeze of the high ridges and corries. One morning, they had set off to penetrate the interior of the wild landscape to the north side of Cul Mor, on the border of Wester Ross and Sutherland. There was a long hike over barren peat moorland, skirting the shores of Loch Sionascaig, before they would reach the higher ground. Midges were active in the mornings as well. As they hurried along the squelching path, waving their arms around their heads in a vain attempt to keep the insects at bay, they passed a farmer tending to repairs to one of the few stone walls across the land. He was not indulging in their antics, but given that he was as surrounded by the mists of blood-sucking fury as the rest of them, there was no doubt that he was as subject to their attention as they were. He smiled at the small group of arm-waving tourists with gentle, kind-hearted sympathy.

"Aye, they're biting today!" he commented as they passed, his soft accent expressing nothing except acceptance of the fact.

As they had hurried across the two miles of boggy ground, Brigg had marvelled at his fortitude, for who knew how long he would be working out there amongst the swarm? For all his subsequent experience of *Culicoides,* Brigg had still not managed to match such stoicism. It was better to run, to wave one's arms about or, better still, to go safely indoors. This late afternoon, he chose the last course of action. Besides, the carers would be there soon.

The carers came and went, sharing kind words and teasing jokes with Marie whilst they changed her pad. Whilst at first she had, understandably, shown a resentment towards them which could manifest itself in aggressive resistance, she was now accepting of their attention and frequently seemed to enjoy their presence. Today, however, she remained passive throughout the change, tired from the exertion of the afternoon.

"Och, the wee lass looks worn out today," one of them remarked to Brigg. "What have you been doing with her, John?"

Brigg smiled and recounted the events of the trip to Dunstaffnage. The carers laughed with him as he told of Marie's total indifference to the potential disaster on the ramp.

"Unshakeable: that's our Marie!" one of them responded. "You'll need a licence to drive that wheelchair, John, if you carry on like that."

Brigg laughed with them, glad of their warmth and still feeling relief that the incident had resulted in such a benign outcome. The carers left, cheerily; they would return in less than three hours to help get Marie ready for the night.

Brigg went back to the kitchen; he would have to get the evening meal ready soon. The monotony of the daily routine, plus the fact that they were now dependent on supermarket deliveries, meant that their diet had become rather restricted. Indeed, to his shame, he tended to use many ready meals; they were almost instant, they could be cooked from frozen and he knew which ones Marie would eat. He would always supplement them with vegetables and fruit, but he could feel the guilt inside him each time he took one out of the freezer. How long-lived were the messages of his upbringing! He would never be worthy. Marie, on the other hand, never seemed to mind, and at least she ate them.

Whilst he was waiting for the microwave to finish the evening's offering, he gazed out at the small back garden where it edged the wilder grass and heather. This time, he did notice the birds on the rowan trees, but his mind was with Marie. He thought of her lying there, either gently sleeping or watching whatever programme was on the television. What kind of life was there left for her? In the beginning, as the condition had begun its insidious degradation, she had fought, she had raged, against the dying of the light. There became two Maries: the afflicted Marie who struggled for words and showed the painful onset of confusion, and the other Marie who stood outside, raging. That Marie had fought the dark, gathering clouds, holding to the central light that was still her, in a vain attempt to hold them at bay. Sometimes fiercely defiant, sometimes consumed with anguish and fear, sometimes lashing out in anger and frustration at those around and at the world in general, she would hold on to the flame of being that made her who she was. But over the years, the degradation had won, as it was certain to do. Specialists argued inconclusively about the causes of PPA, pointing to the build-up of certain proteins in the brain as a factor in the onset of the shrinkage of the cerebral hemispheres and splitting the inadequate definition of the condition itself into three types, but such details only mattered to them. There was no treatment, let alone cure, that would alleviate the symptoms and so sufferers were left in their painful isolation to contend with the inexorable closing of the curtains. For Marie, it had been lonely and at times terrifying; for Brigg, it had simply been heartbreaking. Now, for the most part, the dementia had taken over; the old Marie, the Marie that he knew, that he had married and spent his life with, had gone. Where was she now?

When he himself raged about the injustice and unfairness of the condition he knew there was only one answer to that question. That person did not exist; she had gone, save for a few last flickerings as the candle guttered before it finally went out. He would never have her back. All he had now was the pain of bereavement, bereavement whilst she was still living. Except for isolated flashes of consciousness, such had been brought on by her delight at seeing little Ailsa, the old Marie had died. He would never have her back and Marie would never have herself back. We all die sometime, but not usually whilst we are still alive.

The microwave pinged and he stirred the almost defrosted Chinese meal before putting it back for another few minutes. He switched on the gas under a pan of broccoli; at least there would be some fresh vegetables to assuage his guilt. There was a bizarre strangeness to the living bereavement that he now experienced. The presence of her living body, still warm, still responding, belied the finality of what had happened to the person. But he would care for what was left in her body, for the body was still her; it was, in a way, just another change in the person that was Marie. There had never been a fixed person, an identity separate from her body; as her body had changed through her life, so had the person called Marie. It had been made by her body, by the countless interactions of matter and energy within its structure as it interacted with other bodies and the ideas of the world, whilst maintaining the extraordinary defiance of life in a universe that was running down. The desperate wish of humanity for a separate 'soul' which would have carried her essence in a parallel eternity, was nothing more than a juvenile manifestation of consciousness in a species still searching for the security of its mother's breast. We have seen the outside world, we have looked out of the cave, and we are frightened. We are frightened because our species, alone of all living species and probably sharing it with only a few ancestors, has developed that extraordinary faculty of individual self-consciousness. We see that consciousness threatened by the existence of death. To our perception, living things interact as units and, all around, we see those units die. By extrapolation, we know that reality must apply to us, but we cannot accept the consequences. So we create a fantasy world of gods and spirits and mythical existences where we will carry on even if our bodies endure what seems inevitable. The spiritual nipple of Mother Earth, the embracing arm of God the Father. Stop worrying, stop thinking. Reduce your consciousness of such issues to a gentle acceptance, for it won't be long before you will be in the afterlife – *afterlife?!* – where you can enjoy paradise, Elysian fields, contemplation or virgins for ever, depending on your fancy. What nonsense, and what ironic contradiction of the arrogant nomenclature *Homo sapiens sapiens* has given itself. As individuals, we live and we die with our bodies; and sometimes they kill us before our final demise. Brigg wondered if the religious ever analysed the absurd notions that accompany their sad adherence to the fairytale of an afterlife. Did they really believe, for example, that those who suffer the mind-eating affliction of dementia are suddenly reborn after death with all their faculties intact? *All* their faculties? How would you be sure? At what point could you say that you had all your faculties? At what point in your life are you the 'person' that would be gifted the privilege of eternal life? In what we could call a normal lifespan, if there ever were such a thing, we simply fade away and die; presumably, we have to embark on eternal life with the personality and capability that we have when we die and take the consequences. A bit rough, because you probably weren't feeling too good at that moment of death, but we'll go with it for the moment. However, let's extrapolate to someone with dementia. Are you going to be demented forever? If not, who do we choose out of the myriad 'persons' one has been during one's life? Perhaps it must be the point at which your dementia starts; that intense knowledge of yourself as you are aware that there is something about your body that is degrading: maybe that is the full you. But you've also lost something too, otherwise you wouldn't have dementia. Maybe it must be a little before that, or perhaps just a little before that... And when it's finally all over and you reach the glorious open fields of heaven, does God take you on one side and say 'that was fun, wasn't it? There was never any need to worry, I had a back-up version of you saved all along'? If ever Brigg needed a reason to rage at the incoherent absurdity of religion, he had only to think of poor Marie; poor Marie, whose plight was in the world so that the rest of us would have the opportunity to feel compassion and thus know the loving warmth of Jesus.

Brigg quelled the feelings of exasperation that such reflection always produced and focused on producing the meal for Marie. He strained the broccoli and removed the ready meal from the microwave, transferring half to a bowl, along with a few broccoli florets. He cut the food finely so that it would be easier for her both to chew and to swallow. As he looked out of the window at the late afternoon sun slanting across the gentle moorland, he remembered how difficult life had been for him before he met Marie and how she had, in many ways, saved him from complications in his personal life that had been driving him inexorably into a dead-end. Now, it was as though his adult life had not started until then. He had so much to thank her for. Blinking back the tears, he placed the bowl onto a tray with some cutlery, and took it to Marie's room. She was lying quietly, watching an antiques programme on the television. She looked at him with wide eyes, almost as if in surprise that he had appeared.

"Tea-time", he announced.

*Brigg smiles at Holly, thinking furiously about what to do.*

*"Mmm...a good question, Holly. Where are you indeed? Where, or what, are we, as we construct those images of the world in our consciousness? It's one of those questions that has kept philosophers going for a very long time and I wish I knew. I can tell you some of the ideas that people have had, but I'm afraid I don't have any answers. Where do you think you are?"*

*Holly frowns. "Well, I suppose I'm inside, looking out, at least that's what it feels like."*

*Brigg nods. "Yes, it does, doesn't it? But does that answer your question? What is looking out? Is there a sort of little you inside that is peering through your eyes?"*

*"Well... no..., that's silly," says Holly, hesitantly, "but it's a bit like that, isn't it? I'm sort of on the inside and you're on the outside." Holly purses her lips as she struggles with the idea. She looks hard at Brigg. "This is fascinating, John; I've never, ever thought about it before. We just take it all for granted, don't we?" She looks around at her colleagues. "There's me, and then there's all of you. You're all out there. I'm making all of you up in my brain; just as you must be doing*

*with me. Well, not making you up exactly, but making up what I think I can see of you."*

*She shakes her head in wonder. "It's bonkers." She points at her head. "All of you...are what I'm making up in here... Bonkers," she says again. She looks back at Brigg. "What an interesting session we're having this afternoon, John."*

*Brigg smiles at her and looks at the rest of the group. Some appear to be approaching Holly's conflict light-heartedly; others seem to be much more seriously engaged. Holly is talking earnestly with the students where she is sitting. He lets the conversation flow, conscious of how far the session has moved from his initial extemporisation with Megan. He needs to pull the threads together, building on the kind of wonder that Holly is feeling and somehow give it relevance to their teaching. At the same time, he cannot leave unaddressed the philosophical void he's just opened up. It's very likely that others in the group will be thinking about it as well as Holly. Once again, he feels his own solipsistic intensity: the sense of detachment. He hears Holly's words: "there's me, and then there's all of you...". Everywhere he looks, there is an individual: a unique, experiencing being, fiercely isolated from its neighbour, each in its personal world of consciousness. Some, like Holly, know they inhabit that space; others will be moving through that world with only partial knowledge of where they are. For them, the group remains. But that does not remove the reality of the space. There is only the space for Brigg: his space. Is this what life is? Is he always to be condemned to this isolation?*

*"We need to pull this together," he says, scribbling a few new notes. "I've taken you on a bit of a diversion this afternoon, but I hope you've found it interesting. Our diversion*

*has had two branches: an exploration of how sense organs work and now the rather more involved questions that Holly's just referred to. I think both are useful for you to think about as regards your teaching. First, because it's important that you recognise the science behind your senses, and second, because you have to explore the implications of any ideas and where they might lead. I'm not suggesting that your primary children will ask the sort of questions as Holly, but who knows what kinds of thinking your teaching will trigger? Teachers often fall into the rather arrogant position of assuming that children will think the ideas that they impart to them; that if the lesson is about* x, *the children will think about* x, *not* y, *or* x *and* y. *If you are sitting there now, thinking about all sorts of things, then why won't the children in your classroom? No-one knows what goes on inside the mind of someone else; all we can do is extrapolate from our own experience, coupled with a hopeful understanding of the ways young minds develop.*

*"So, it's not for me to tell you what to think about this session. I hope, like Holly, you've found it interesting. I wanted to take the opportunity of doing something a little bit exploratory before you are thrust into the very necessary, but potentially stifling world of planning, targets and the National Curriculum. I think we've covered some of the main things to think about when analysing how the senses work, and I think Holly's just shown how thinking about science can raise all sorts of fascinating philosophical questions." He smiles at her. "I won't finish without making a couple of suggestions about your question, but the bottom line is that I can't give you an answer. As I said, it's kept philosophers going for over two thousand years."*

*Brigg looks out of the window at the lighted buildings spread across the campus, hurriedly sorting out a plethora of ideas that are vying for position in his brain. Turning to the computer, he opens up the course programme, finding a table that he had placed in the student reference material. He knows how he will proceed.*

*"But before that," he continues, "something of more direct relevance to your teaching. For a moment, I want to consider how we got to where we are now, from where we started this afternoon. In a way, we have just gone through a microcosm of how young children's thinking develops. When I first asked you to tell me how you could see Megan, you answered immediately, with common sense, intuitive understanding. It wasn't until we explored those intuitive ideas that we began to develop a deeper, more sophisticated perspective. Now, let's think about young children; very young children who are just starting school. In fact, let's go back even further, to earliest infancy."*

*He glances around the group and is pleased to see that they are engaged. They have entered what he always thinks of as 'lecture mode': notepads out, pens at the ready, waiting to be filled up with words of wisdom. His ridiculously overactive brain starts thinking about the moral and ethical implications for people in his position; how whatever he says must be honest, measured and justifiable. In this mode, content goes in before there is any interaction with higher processes and he is not there to inculcate. He brings himself back to the task in hand; he feels confident of his ground.*

*"Think about a new born baby. It is utterly helpless physically, dependent on its mother for all its needs. It is also, I would suggest, not yet conscious. The person it is to become is*

*yet to develop. It is sensitive to pain, yes, but its brain has yet to start the process of sorting and filtering, comparing and cataloguing the sensory bombardment it is suddenly receiving. Only when it does so, will the conscious personality emerge."*

*He looks around again, anticipating that some will resist the idea, but there is no reaction. He continues:*

*"As it grows and the brain starts that long process of maturation, the infant becomes immersed in events. Things happen to it; it does things. Visual stimuli, auditory stimuli, textures, surfaces, tastes, smells; they bathe the developing child in the wonderful complexity of its surroundings. It doesn't think about these stimuli in the way you and I as adults might do; in order to that, it would have to be able to stand back and relate experience to a bank of ideas. No, it is immersed in the moment; it is not even having experiences – yet. But out of that immersion in events there arises the beginning of self; the single most astounding potential of the human brain. With self, events become personalised: they become experience, and with experience, the way is open for the development of ideas. To begin with, these emergent ideas are intuitive. They are ideas based on how things feel; automatic responses deriving from unexamined patterns and relationships, not on speculation. The infant mind is animistic and anthropomorphic; toys have names and teddy bears have feelings that are just as real as yours are. Talk to four and five year olds; the boundaries between the concrete Here and Now and the quasi-magical world of books and fairytales are blurred.*

*"Intuitive ideas are useful and, in some circumstances, very tenacious, as your immediate responses to the problem of sight were. It feels as though we see by looking out from our eyes at the world, not by receiving light energy from it with*

*them. It takes thought, speculation, enquiry and comparison of different perspectives, before we can understand what seems really to be going on and trigger those bigger questions that Holly is hinting at. However, although they may not be scientifically accurate, intuitive ideas make sense to us and I would suggest that as adults we employ intuitive thinking throughout a large proportion of our everyday life. Intuitive ideas work; they allow us to navigate our way through the world. It's only when they don't work that we become aware of them. Software producers spend a lot of their time trying to ensure that their products are intuitive and I'm sure I'm not the only one who gets annoyed with a program when I have to think my way through mouse clicks or swipes, rather than just following paths which 'feel' natural.*

*"However, as teachers, it is part of our job to help children develop their nascent ability to be rational. We know that it is our responsibility to help them unlock that potential, the potential that makes them human; the privilege that they're born with. We must be careful how we do it; there is a pattern to children's development which we can't rush, but that doesn't mean to say we can't stimulate it.*

*"As children reach the age of about five or so, they are developing the natural ability and tendency to stand back from their experience and to focus in a different way on everyday phenomena. They are now not just noticing things; they are beginning to notice that they are noticing. It's a crucial stage; it's the beginning of what we could call true observation. It's about generating an awareness of themselves in the world. That's why we make the development of children's observation centrally important in our science teaching, and it underpins so much else at that age. It's not just about them acquiring ideas;*

*in a way it's even more important. It's helping them to develop their consciousness."*

*Brigg scans the students. "But of course, it does promote ideas as well – rational ideas. How did we start to explore the way we could see Megan, once we'd trawled around for our intuitive ideas?"*

*"You got us to observe her carefully, John," Amanda replies immediately.*

*"Exactly. And those observations led us quickly to a much more sophisticated understanding of how sight works, based first on comparison between them, but then on to the implications of other ideas that we've picked up through education or elsewhere.*

*"That's what I mean about what we did being a microcosm of how children develop. We already had a lot of ideas about sight and other relevant areas of biology and physics, but, as we saw, they were not fully incorporated into our everyday intuitive consciousness about perception. Young children, of course, don't yet have those ideas, or the capability for understanding them, but they have already had a range of experiences which we can help them explore. As they do, they will also begin to use them as we did, moving from intuitive to rational processing. That's what we have to be aiming at in our science teaching."*

*Brigg sends the table in the electronic notes through to the interactive whiteboard. It references general themes in the development and progression of young children's cognitive and processing abilities in areas that are central to their future learning in science. The students gaze at it, fully immersed in their own 'lecture mode'. There is something so secure in the sensation of switching off the slightly disconcerting tension that an interactive session produces and slipping into the passive mode of receiving a presentation... He continues:*

*"I'm not going to go through this in detail now, but I wanted to draw it to your attention. It's in your programme notes. The important part for us now is the top line: the one that deals with children's ideas and their relation to the child's developing cognitive ability. I would suggest to you that it is probably one of the most important strands of development that any of us ever go through. We are not just dealing with knowledge-formation, we are involved with the emergence of an individual's self-awareness. That's why teaching is one of the most important jobs you could choose: you are dealing with the futures of individual people.*

*"There seems to be a cycle or, more accurately, a spiral, of development in thinking that is going on in the infant and primary years, which is then mirrored in the secondary; one that really helps to make sense of your science teaching, and much of the rest of it too. We start with infant children who are located in the Here and Now, and whose thinking is immersed in immediate experience. We might write on our planning sheets that they're dealing with Forces; the children are focused on how they can get their car to go fast."*

*"It's really important you remember that. The ideas that seven-year-olds are generating are concrete; these cars, these surfaces. Some of them will be able to start applying their findings to other situations, but their thinking is located in that concrete experience; it will be those cars, those surfaces. We can be so guilty of trying to impose an abstract understanding on them. And please don't assume that just because they can start to come up with a concrete generalisation at seven, they must be ready for abstract ideas by nine or ten. Some might be,*

*but very many, probably the majority, won't. Intuitive ideas will still abound – we saw how we all still have them as adults – and I'm sure a lot of you found the abstract physics ideas you had to deal with six years later at GCSE hard to understand. However, if we get our teaching right, by the end of primary school the children should have had the opportunity to explore their concrete experience in all the areas we, as adults, categorise in abstract terms like Forces or Materials. In that way, there's never a distance between the thinking they are developing and their intuitive ideas; we are always working from their experience."*

*He smiles. "Don't tell Ofsted, but I don't particularly care whether an eleven-year-old can tell me about gravity and that it's got something to do with the Earth pulling things down, because she won't have a clue as to what that means. What I care about is that she can explore the phenomenon of things falling, observing carefully what happens in different places, with different things, and then has the ability to relate those observations to each other and come up with ideas about what might be going on, based securely on what she has seen. Why should she know about gravity? I'll bet most of you would be hard pushed to come up with a good explanation of it."*

*Brigg is pleased to hear a ripple of ironic laughter among the students. At least he's still got their attention.*

*"But, of course," he continues, "we do gently introduce the idea of gravity in Key Stage Two, for it adds to their own cataloguing of experience; and if they've had the opportunity for focused concrete experience, it will make much more sense to them. As their ability to stand back develops, so does their ability to bring in ideas that are not based in the Here and Now. We get them to share ideas and explanations for their own*

*experiences so they can explore them further, so introducing an idea like gravity is simply expanding that principle. But there's no rush."*

*He sighs. "Yes, I know you've got all sorts of conceptual targets for them by seven, or eleven, and of course you've got to teach them. But don't expect understanding of them unless you've helped the children to think by letting their procedural understanding develop, so they also have the opportunity to explore them. We all carry around so much in the way of snippets of knowledge that we can repeat, but have absolutely no understanding of.*

*"Development across the secondary ages mirrors the development in the primary, just one revolution further up the spiral. Children will move from having a bank of linked concrete ideas which they've derived from handling their experience consistently, to being able to relate those concrete ideas to abstract science ideas, and starting to see links between those. Or at least they should; we know from experience that it certainly doesn't happen in all cases... From a cognitive perspective, from the point of view of their developing rationality and consciousness, that's what moving towards the Piagetian goal of formal operations means. However," Brigg adds, "many will not reach that by the end of secondary school or, at most, reach it only partially."*

*He switches off the whiteboard. "Anyway, that's the general idea; have a think about it and we can pick up on any questions at another time."*

*The students are still fully immersed in their passive receptivity. However, Vicky finishes scribbling some notes and looks quizzically at Brigg.*

*"I can see what you're getting at, John, but I can't just ignore all those knowledge targets in the curriculum. I've still got to teach them."*

*Brigg nods. "Yes, of course you have, I realise that. I know that at times you will also feel that you've just got to tell children things so that they can repeat it for SATs, or just so you can feel you've covered your curriculum responsibilities. I'm not saying that introducing ideas from the outside is wrong; in fact, it can be extremely valuable and I'm sure you can all remember being filled with excitement when you came across certain ideas. They can really stimulate thinking and you will have some children whose minds will be ready. We mustn't forget that they are there and should be prepared to accommodate them. What I am saying is don't lose sight of the overall principles for, as principles, they apply across the board, sometimes earlier in development, sometimes later. Remember also, that bits of knowledge are transient: what you learn in primary school will be superseded in secondary and that, in turn, will very probably be inadequate, or often plain wrong, if you were to go on to study it further in higher education. Yes, children need to remember snippets of knowledge; but repeating parrot-fashion is not the same as understanding. Unfortunately, I've seen so many classrooms in which, because of a teacher's inadequacy, that becomes the main focus of their science teaching. What I'm trying to say to you is that there's a bigger picture that you shouldn't lose sight of."*

*Vicky purses her lips. "Okay... but it's difficult John."*

*Some of the students mutter to each other; others sit quietly, as if waiting for Brigg to go on. He decides not to pursue Vicky's disquiet any further, otherwise he will run out of time.*

*"Yes, I know it is, Vicky. I haven't got time to say any more at the moment, if we are to deal with Holly's question as well before the end of the session, but you can always find me for a chat, if you want to talk about it more. We'll also cover it in more practical detail next time when we look at planning."*

*He looks over at Holly, who, like the rest of the students, seems to have been immersed in lecture mode, but who has not lost the intensity in her expression. She returns his gaze, and Brigg notices she has large, attractive, brown eyes. He had not noticed them before or, rather, he had not noticed that he had noticed them before. He smiles at her. He had long ago decided that, far from being unique, faces, at least the majority white faces that seemed to populate the teaching courses, could be differentiated into about seven different kinds. Year on year, as new students arrived, he would scan them and be mildly amused that another set of potential doppelgangers would be challenging his increasingly overloaded capacity for name-recognition. With so many to cope with, it was inevitable that he would be unsuccessful in many cases, leading to various levels of embarrassment as he struggled to return cheery personal greetings. It was so much easier for the students: they would meet at the maximum only fifteen to twenty lecturers, whilst he had at least a hundred new faces each year to contend with. The problem was exacerbated by the nature of the programme. Because it incorporated professional training within traditional university study, much of the contact between lecturer and student was in smaller, interactive groups rather than large lectures. The tone of these groups was personal and much depended on professional relationships. There was a strong element of modelling of professional interaction by the lecturer. The more that interaction flowed, the more it was dependent on the use of first names and a natural interplay of conversation, questioning and humour. It was no wonder that the students would perhaps be rather surprised if, only a few hours after such a session, where Brigg had been talking freely and personally to them, he might struggle to remember any of their names.*

*Holly smiles back. Brigg thinks for a moment, sorting out what he's going to say and glances at his watch. There is not a great deal of time left. He needs to be as concise as possible. There's no question of overrunning; the room will be needed at five. He continues:*

*"Okay, we've not got much longer, but I did promise I'd try to give Holly some kind of answer to her question which, as I understand it, concerns the nature of the 'I' that is processing all the sense data we've been talking about: the 'I' that we feel is looking out of our eyes as we scan the world." He looks at her for confirmation. "Is that the sort of thing you were getting at?"*

*Holly nods. "Yes. It's odd, isn't it? When you become aware of it, it makes you feel detached from everything."*

*Brigg quells his own raging sense of detachment. "Mmm," he agrees, "I suppose it does."*

*He addresses the rest of the group. "Do you feel what Holly is referring to?"*

*There are affirmative murmurs all around the room.*

*"It's weird when you focus on it," says Ben, looking serious.*

*Brigg nods. "Yes," he says quietly, "very."*

*"Maybe you're all just figments of my imagination!" chortles another male student, Damian, who is sitting at a table at the far end of the room.*

*There is laughter around the room, but Brigg notices Holly looks annoyed.*

*"Yeah, but what does that mean?" she asks tersely.*

*Damian shrugs. "Oh, I don't know; it's just what people say, isn't it? It seems to be what John's implying; I haven't really thought about it."*

*"That's the point," says Holly; "nor had I. But it's fascinating when you do."*

*Her tone quietens the group. Ben looks up at Brigg. "So, what do you think, John?" he asks.*

*"I agree with you," he replies.*

*"What, that it's weird?"*

*"Yes."*

*"So where is it?"*

*"I don't know," says Brigg, "not a clue"*

*He sees the frustration in Ben's expression.*

*"But I empathise completely with what Holly said about it feeling as though someone inside is looking out through my eyes."*

*"Well, it certainly feels as though it's in my head," says Holly; "presumably it's somewhere in my brain. It must be if all that processing is going on there." She stops, looking quizzically at Brigg. "Doesn't it have something to do with your soul, though? Surely that's the bit that is the real me?"*

*Brigg purses his lips. "Now that is a question...," he says slowly. "Of course, not everybody would accept the idea that you have a soul, but let's put that issue to one side for a moment. Let's start with thinking about the first part of what you just said. It seems logical to think of the 'I' as in our head; perhaps it is. Do you think it still feels like that if you're blind? Maybe we think of it in that way because we rely so heavily on our sight and our eyes are in our head. I don't know, but it certainly seems to be a question which is bound up with the nature of our perception. After all, there's presumably a difference between sensing something, which we say is a feature of all living things, and perceiving: knowing that I am sensing something."*

*Brigg frowns thoughtfully at Holly. "I don't think I can help much with answering your question, because individual consciousness is the most difficult question of all and I've not yet found a convincing explanation of it from anyone. However, what I can do is give a quick overview of some philosophical positions regarding ways of looking the nature of things; they all have implications for understanding consciousness. Do you think that would help? Considering what we have been talking about this afternoon, I think it would finish off the session well."*

*Holly nods. "I'm sure that would be interesting, thank you."*

*Brigg looks at the rest of the group. "Is that okay with you all?" he asks. "I'll just do a quick whizz through about three thousand years of philosophy. Well, perhaps not quite that much, but whatever I say is obviously going to be very simplistic."*

*There are murmurs of agreement through the group.*

*Brigg continues. "Let's say for starters that Damian actually wasn't wide of the mark with his comment; it may be an extreme position, but a perfectly valid one to take, so long as you can justify it."*

*He winks at Damian; Damian grins.*

*"It might just bring us back to that question of whether it's mind or matter. Do we as conscious people, inhabit a*

*separate place which we might call our mind, or is mind simply a function of the matter of our bodies? As I said earlier, if you wanted to put labels on them, the first is more of what is known as an Idealist position, the second a Materialist one.*

*"We're in a science session and science is about the material world, so we'll take the second one first. At its heart, materialism says that the physical world is all there is and so our consciousness must be a product of the way the physical world works. Don't look for an external entity like mind; there's no such thing. A materialist would say that we have consciousness because something about the way we have evolved has given our brains the capacity to generate conscious awareness. We know we have extraordinarily complex brains, so why shouldn't our consciousness simply be the icing on the cake of that aspect of our evolution? If you look at it that way, your consciousness is almost a bonus on top of all the other things your brain can do. Somehow, that phenomenal complexity of structure and wiring in the brain can produce a process that is aware of itself. And why not? A materialist would say, with considerable justification, that to go looking for anything else is futile: there is no evidence for anything existing apart from the physical world. The answers must lie there. We know that conscious states can be explored by looking at brain waves, so there must be a correlation. We also know that consciousness degrades when brains degrade; think of people who suffer from dementia. If it is that kind of physical process, it does sort of explain why we think our 'I' is located somewhere in our heads, and looking out at the world."*

*Brigg glances at Ben; he is following what Brigg is saying with an expression of deep concentration on his face. Brigg nods at him and then continues:*

*"Thinking about Ben's question earlier, the question that follows automatically from that reasoning is whether humans are indeed the only conscious creatures on the planet. If consciousness is a result of brain evolution, at what point in evolution did it arise? Is it all or nothing? Are there, perhaps, grades of consciousness amongst animals, with humans just having the most complex, as far as we know? All fascinating questions, with possibly disturbing consequences.*

*"A philosopher that you might want to take a look at if you're interested, is a chap called David Chalmers. He's an Australian but working in America. He's quite heavy going, but he is particularly interested in the question of what mechanism could produce conscious awareness out of the physical interactions of matter: energy transfers and so on. He does not dismiss the idea, but he has formulated his unease as a kind of challenge to materialists. He calls it the 'hard problem' of consciousness: how can non-conscious matter generate conscious, subjective awareness. He suggests it's up to materialists to show how it is possible. If no-one can solve it, it means that the model we've been discussing is missing something: a sort of magical bridge from sensory input to the kicking-in of awareness. Interesting, to say the least.*

*"There is, however, another philosopher who is also making a name for himself in this area. He is Daniel Dennett, also in America. He's at one extreme of the materialist continuum, but his analysis is detailed and many would say it is logical and consistent, although it is rather controversial. He objects to the implicit idea in Chalmers' hard problem that consciousness is a thing, something we could find if we went looking for it. Dennett suggests that consciousness as such does not exist at all; it is an illusion. There isn't a thing that we can*

*isolate as consciousness; it is an illusion generated, as it were, by the layer upon layer of neural processes in human brains. As they fire in their complex way, the conscious feeling is produced and it switches off when we're not using it. It doesn't change your experience of being conscious, but it's no more a thing than a damn good peristaltic wave in your gut in the morning. It's what your body does, or can do."*

*Some students who realise what he's referring to smile or laugh quietly. Brigg looks quizzically at them all. "Make sense? It might affront your sensibilities, but that's not enough to reject it out of hand.*

*"Dennett would say he has solved Chalmers' problem by suggesting that consciousness is just an illusion but, as I said, he is at the extreme of the materialist continuum and there are many materialists who are perhaps more challenged by it".*

*He glances again at his watch; he's doing okay for time.*

*"Okay, in a nutshell, that's the materialist idea. Let's now have a quick look at the other end of our continuum and the idea that consciousness is something to do with a completely different kind of existence from matter, called mind. Some philosophers take the idea to an extreme and suggest that actually it is matter that is the illusion and that everything is a product of that feature of existence we call mind. That is the fully idealist position, and note that it is not to do with what we normally think of as ideals. They're different; they're about aims and aspirations.*

*"Idealism as an understanding of consciousness is to do with the realisation that our sensations and perceptions, as we have been finding out when we were analysing what we could see of Megan, seem to be ideas we generate for ourselves. Idealism in philosophy really started with the eighteenth-*

*century Irish scholar and clergyman, Bishop Berkeley. He looked at the way we perceive things and suggested that, as the qualities of objects, such as warmth, or colour, or taste, or smell vary from person to person, they can't be real properties of the things themselves. They only exist in the way we perceive them."*

*"What, so hot water isn't really hot?" asks Becky, frowning.*

*"No, not really. It may feel hot to you at the time, but that's because you are measuring it against yourself. The hottest water is only about a hundred degrees Celsius before it vaporises, which is pretty cool when you think of molten iron, or the surface of the Sun."*

*Brigg can see that Becky is not convinced. "If you don't believe me," he says, "there's a great little demonstration of how not even your own body can make up its mind what's hot or cold. You can do it with older children in the primary school, to get them talking and thinking. Get three bowls of water, one as hot as you can take, one room temperature and one as cold as you can. Put your left hand in the cold and the right one in the hot for twenty seconds or so. Then take them out and put them in the room temperature bowl. Your left hand will think the water is warm, the right hand will think it's cold. Your brain doesn't know what quality to attribute to the water; it's cold and hot at the same time!"*

*Becky has turned away and is talking to the students at her table. Brigg raises his voice a little to signify that they have to keep going.*

*"Those were the kinds of experiences that Berkeley was referring to. He also held a central philosophical principle, which was that for something to exist, it must be able to be*

*perceived. But if what we perceived was subjective, it left him a problem, which he resolved by concluding that the only things we can actually say are real are the 'ideas' we have of things in our minds. From that, we get the common saying that Damian came up with: that things are just a 'figment of my imagination'. This kind of idealism doesn't have to dispense with the material world as such; it's more about what we can know about it. Another, perhaps even more important eighteenth-century philosopher, Immanuel Kant, refined the idea, trying to be more precise about what was objective in our perception, rather than just what we might be imagining. He ended up with ideas that were a little bit like those we've had today. He claimed that all our perceptions, all the ways that things appear to us, are merely mental representations inside us. They cannot give us access to what he called 'things-in-themselves'. From this, he extrapolated that everything we think we perceive about things, including their existing in time and space, is merely the product of the way our minds work and not of the things in themselves. To all intents and purposes, the world we experience is in our minds."*

*He pauses for a moment; he wants to emphasise the point. "If you think about what we were saying about our senses this afternoon and what we really knew of where Megan was, it sounds a bit similar, doesn't it?*

*"Berkeley and Kant weren't denying that there could be a material world, but they suggested it was always destined to be hidden from us. However, others during the nineteenth century, like Schopenhauer, took the idea even further, and that has led to the fully idealist position that some hold today, where there is no physical world at all and that all that exists is a product of minds, in other words, consciousness. Some,*

*making connections with Eastern religious and philosophical ideas, claim that our individual consciousness is merely part of a single, overarching mind or consciousness that underpins everything.*

*"Sounds a bit like God," says Ben.*

*"You may say that, I couldn't possibly comment..." Brigg replies, smiling. He continues:*

*"The trouble with exploring the problem of consciousness is that in the end everybody seems to tie themselves in knots. I've got a feeling that the two camps of materialism and idealism are a bit phoney, but I'm not sure if we're equipped to make sense of it at all. Somewhat paradoxically, some idealists find evidence to support their ideas in the strange and uncertain world that is being described by quantum physics, in which the very notion of substance in the way we have intuitively perceived it becomes meaningless."*

*He shrugs "I say paradoxically, because quantum physics is a materialist theory. Obviously, I haven't got time to go into that now, and even if I had, it wouldn't get us very far. My understanding of quantum physics is rudimentary to say the least. I wouldn't know what I was talking about. I'm just putting forward some ideas for you to go away and think about. A discussion for another time, perhaps.*

*"Okay, we've not got much time left now. I said at the beginning that we seemed to have two options: mind or matter. As I'm sure you've probably worked out, there is in fact a third option, and it's quite possibly the one that you hold; it's certainly the most common one if you were to ask people. It's what Holly was referring to a moment ago when she mentioned the idea of a soul. It's known as dualism. It's an amalgam of the other two, and a kind of extension of where*

*Berkeley and Kant had got to. It suggests that that reality actually consists of two separate, but interacting parts, one of which is the material world, the other something intangible, maybe what we call mind, where consciousness lies. Some would say it's the most intuitive position to hold. As a philosophical position, it's called dualism because it proposes two kinds of stuff, rather than the single stuff suggested by pure materialists or idealists. That's called monism. You may hear something referred to as Cartesian Dualism, after the seventeenth century scientist and philosopher Rene Descartes, who tried systematically to explore the nature of existence. You will all, I am sure, know of his famous saying: 'I think, therefore I am'. To simplify dualism, it places consciousness in the mind, which is a separate element of reality from matter. In religious terms, it becomes the 'soul' or 'spirit' which inhabits everyone and which is not contingent upon the demise of the body. As a philosophical tradition, it occupies a central place in deliberations about the nature of consciousness, postulating that mind cannot be explained simply by consideration of the physical processes of matter, but it does not deny that matter exists. That makes it fit in with Berkeley's and Kant's ideas and does away with Chalmers' hard problem. Descartes started the ball rolling when he suggested that if you're trying to work out what actually exists, the only thing we can use as a starting point for our analysis is the one experience we think we can be certain of: the fact that we exist. We know of that, because we are thinking, hence his famous saying. Cogito, ergo sum. Thinking is a mental process, hence the idea of mind.*

*"Some dualists see consciousness and matter as being separate, others think that consciousness or mind is somehow a sort of non-material property of matter. There is a dualist idea*

*called panpsychism which tries to explain from an evolutionary perspective how consciousness has developed, by suggesting that consciousness is actually present in everything, including rocks and stones as well as primitive living things. The idea is that, as evolution has progressed and complexity increased, consciousness has slowly built up until it has generated what we could call a critical mass, producing the self-reflective awareness that we experience. As an idea, it gets around the hard problem, but it doesn't actually say what consciousness is."*

*Brigg laughs. "It gives flatworms a chance, though! However, it's also a little difficult to see how it works. Surely it could mean that elephants and blue whales would be more conscious than us? They're bigger." He shrugs. "Maybe they are...*

*"However," he continues, "It's easy to see that most of the world's religions adopt a dualist perspective, particularly the Abrahamic traditions of Christianity, Islam and Judaism. It would certainly be difficult to have an afterlife if there were only matter. Even if you are not religious, you will, I am sure, recognise how much the dualist idea permeates our culture, from the establishment of the Church and the assumption of the Divine in the great formal occasions of the constitution, to the popularity of ghosts, spirits and messing about at Halloween. Many people consider that people have souls and it's there that their minds reside for all eternity; the body being merely a temporary housing that will pass away. Again, no hard problem any more: consciousness is in the mind, the soul. You don't have to be religious to be this kind of dualist, and I would suggest that our cultural immersion in the idea makes it*

*more likely you hold that kind of perspective even if you are not."*

*Brigg relaxes; he has covered as much ground as he wanted. Very superficial, yes, but at least he has not let Holly's comment pass unaddressed. Holly Is, in fact, talking earnestly to her companions and there is a good buzz of conversation around the room. After his brief immersion in lecturing, Brigg feels his detachment again. As he was speaking, he had been one with the common enterprise of the group, losing his own identity for a moment; but now he has delivered. They have become other again. He looks again at Holly. She appears satisfied with his exposition; she still has the bright, animated expression she had earlier. Brigg knows he hasn't really answered her question, but in reality, he doesn't have an answer at all.*

*"Okay, let's just round it off before we finish," he says, getting the students' attention again. "I hope that's given you something to think about, Holly, but in a way, I know I've not really answered your question. All three perspectives are really third-party descriptions of what the world might be, rather than that question of where* you *are. There is a paradox about consciousness that I'm not sure any of them address. We only ever experience the world from our individual perspective, we are always separate; I'm not sure if any of the three perspectives can explain that sensation fully. The dualist idea encompasses your idea of a soul, but it doesn't explain what that is, or where it is. In a way, the mystery is still just as strong."*

*He looks away from Holly at the whole group. "But thank you all for a fascinating session this afternoon, I've really enjoyed it and I hope you have too. The fact that we've arrived at some highly philosophical ideas simply by taking a deeper look at how our sense organs work, reinforces in my mind just how powerful science can be, if we remember that, at its heart, it is simply a manifestation of the human capacity for enquiry. In the past, the procedures of science were subsumed within the overall idea of 'Natural Philosophy' and I see no reason why one should not continue to think of it in that way."*

*He glances at the door. He can see students gathering outside for the next session in the room.*

*"We'd better leave it now," he says, "we're going to be thrown out in a minute." He smiles. "Next time, we can focus on some really interesting stuff: we're looking at planning..."*

*The students gather their notepads and there is a scraping of chairs and an increase in the volume of talk and interaction as they don coats and bags and head for the door. Holly is still talking animatedly with her friends, but she smiles at Brigg as she passes.*

*"Thank you, John; that was really interesting."*

*Brigg smiles back.*

*"Lots of things to think about, and no answers!"*

*Holly laughs, and is out of the door, still deep in conversation. Ben is one of the last to leave. He is still looking serious.*

*"Where do you stand on all of that, John?" he asks*

*Brigg knows he wants to talk further, but now is not the time.*

*"I actually don't know," he replies honestly. "But I'll say this: I think one of those perspectives is absurd. Have a think about it and we can talk at another time, but we've got to finish now."*

*He turns away and gathers up his own notes. Ben looks perplexed, but reluctantly takes the hint and walks on to the door.*

*Members of the next tutorial group are already coming into the room, accompanied by a lecturer Brigg has not seen before. Many different programmes use the same teaching rooms. Brigg nods at her in acknowledgement.*

*"Hope I haven't kept you waiting."*

*She smiles. "Not a problem. Whatever you were talking about, it seems to have been a success; they seem really engaged. I hope my session goes as well!"*

*Brigg gives a short laugh. "Nice for it to work sometimes; I'm sure yours will be brilliant." He looks around the room. "I don't think we've left it in too much of a mess."*

*Her students are already sitting in the recently vacated chairs.*

*"Don't worry, it's fine," she says, sorting out her notes.*

*The knowledge mill grinds on, thinks Brigg, and leaves.*

The long-term consequences of the trip to Dunstaffnage slowly became absorbed into their daily routine. After Marie had settled back into the gentle comfort of the inflatable pressure mattress and relaxed before the soothing monotony of the television, she could not be stimulated, encouraged, cajoled, badgered or anything else into leaving her bed again. Somewhere, deep in her psyche, she had switched off from the outside world. Whether the sight of the loch from the window was sufficient to assuage the yearning for the natural world that is part of our animal being, or that this desire had simply faded away, no-one would ever know. But as the days passed into weeks, Brigg realised that this was to be the new reality. Another step along a road to who knew where. Her body was tired. Even before the PPA, the CMT had meant that life had always been a struggle; now, the cumulative effect of the car sickness, the incident on the ramp, the strain of being lifted back and forth into the wheelchair and the sheer loss of muscle tone from months of lying down, was that her body was finally rebelling. They moved into a new routine, an extension of the old one, but one in which the prospect of any escape from the house was now lost.

When does solitude become loneliness? Or can a forced isolation lead not to loneliness but a relaxation into an acceptance of the stark fact that, despite our constant attempts at denial, we are all, inescapably, alone. In a strange paradox, Brigg found that the longer he was confined to the house, the less he now yearned for company. Lachlan and Eilidh did bring Ailsa for a visit one afternoon and he enjoyed their company for a couple of hours, but when they had gone, he slipped back into the calm rhythm of the isolation of his life. He spoke regularly to his children via internet video conferencing and both made the journey to see them during that summer, along with some other family members and two friends. It was, of course, wonderful to see them all and he felt the distance he and Marie had placed between them all. But, as his son said, we all make decisions about where to live and it would not be right for one person's choices to determine another's. They all knew they could be together when wanted, or needed; one day's travel was hardly a barrier. Perhaps not for them, but the new circumstances meant it was different for Brigg. He had always been of his son's mind; he had never felt daunted by distance and had regularly driven from the South for visits to the north Highlands, thinking nothing of a twelve-hour car journey. Indeed, he enjoyed the drive almost as much as the arrival and it gave him the reassurance when he was away from them that his beloved Highlands were always easily within reach. Britain really was a small island, which made the wish of some of its inhabitants to divide it into even smaller units seem absurd. But now a subtle difference had insinuated itself into his mind-set. Although the car stood outside waiting, his freedom to travel had been removed and the equanimity that came from knowing he could travel if wanted or needed had been eroded. On both his children's visits, he selfishly took advantage of their presence to take the car out for a short drive. The landscape had never felt so sweet. When no-one was around, he was reduced to running the car every few days to keep the battery topped-up, moving it backwards and forwards so that the pressure on the tyres varied, and dreaming.

Had he ceased being lonely? As social apes, human beings have a genetic predisposition towards contact with others of their kind. A single chimp, or gorilla, is a sorry sight: it needs its companions for survival and mental stability. But the potential intensity of human self-reflection allows us to explore the nature of that drive towards society we all still feel. Society for society's sake has gone: humans choose their society, even to the point of deciding that it may be better to have none rather than those which are on offer. For Brigg at this moment, it had often become better to have none. The parameters of his isolation had generated a state of necessary self-sufficiency, manifesting in daily routines which had fallen into strict patterns. The patterns themselves began to hold security within them, allowing his mind to detach and to occupy a parallel existence separate from the physical needs of his world. Within that parallel space, he could clear his consciousness of much of the clutter that normally pervaded it, allowing him to accept the monotonous regularity of the new house-bound life with Marie without a constant sense of deprivation. The advent of visitors became a disturbance to this world. They would interfere with routines, breaking the detachment, producing irritation and forcing him to focus on the trivial, making him look forward to the moment he could re-establish control. Only the closest family could transcend the annoyance with social contact that ensued and bring him back into the warmth of the innate primate urge for his kind. He was, in effect, displaying all the classic signs of a recluse. It was not a state he sought, but it maintained his mental stability during the silent days and weeks.

Yet within this detached existence, he was increasingly content. The days passed in their routine monotony, but there was no monotony in his mental life. Each day, the world was different. The seasons changed subtly, in ways he would normally have missed. Different birds came to the garden or flew overhead; the water in the loch turned from grey to blue as the sun played with the clouds hovering over Cruachan. Sometimes, often for days, the hills would be obscured as the rain came in from the West, replenishing the burns and making the sloping garden slippery and treacherous. Occasionally, a skein of greylag geese would fly overhead, their constant honking declaring most emphatically that social isolation was not for them. Within the gentle appreciation of these deeper rhythms to the world, he became content with himself. The initial frustration of quasi house-arrest dissipated and he began to be aware of the calmness that was developing. The thought of Marie was, of course, a constant, but he had no control over her plight and she now became part of the circumstances of his world that had to be accepted for what they were. From Marie to the birds, from his neighbours to the loch and the clouds, that world was always outside him; he would forever be alone. The social drive only masked that fact. Yet the more aware of his isolation he became, the closer he felt to all things. The rhythms of the world were inside him; his consciousness could no more be separate from those rhythms than could his head from his body. Whatever it was, the world determined his being. Out of not-him he had arrived and to not-him he would return, not diminished but contributory to existence, of which he was a fundamental part. If there is a meaning to life at all, it must surely lie in that recognition of our own integrity and the development of calm acceptance of its finite bounds. It will pass when we pass, but whilst we have it, it is a wonder of extraordinary magnificence. At the deep, quiet times, Brigg felt that wonder and had no fear of his solitude. There is always meaning in the world, but the meaning we feel is a human meaning. We see patterns, we see rhythms, we see past, present and future; we see design, we see development; we see ecology, we see evolution; we see progression, we see cycles; we see change, we see deep, silent stasis. It brings warmth and consolation to the finite bounds of our lives. But where humanity deludes itself is when it tries to attach Meaning to that meaning. The world doesn't mean anything. Existence generates itself each moment; no past, no future: just now.

The visit of Lachlan, Eilidh and Ailsa had been very pleasant and Marie had for a short while been delighted to see Ailsa again. For perhaps ten minutes, Ailsa had entertained her with giggles and funny faces, enjoying pressing the buttons of the bed control to send Marie up and down. But the little girl had soon tired. Ten minutes for a two-year-old is akin to at least half an hour of adult time. Marie could do nothing to enhance her game with the buttons and so her attention soon passed to exploring other items around the room, with predictable outcomes as she picked up all sorts of inappropriate items and tangled herself up in the wires to the bed. Marie herself had also soon tired once Ailsa went elsewhere. She had drifted back to the television, a reassuring constant in the corner of her room, turning away from them all. Brigg had anticipated it, but it was still saddening, emphasising just how much the dementia had changed her. In the past, it had always been Marie who had sought out their social contact. After the obligatory biscuits and cup of tea, Brigg took their three guests out into the front garden, where Ailsa proceeded to enjoy a game of sliding down the slight hill whilst her mother kept her safe, and he and Lachlan talked about the view, the loch and the hills. But the game could not last for long, for Ailsa again wanted new stimuli and the midges would be returning as the pleasant breeze that had blown all day dropped. It soon became apparent to them all that it was time to leave. Although they parted with all good intentions to maintain contact, Brigg had not yet seen them again, although he had exchanged one or two messages. He did not mind, nor did he blame them; there was little there for them as a family. Once she had turned away from them in the room, Marie showed no further interest, although Brigg knew she would be stimulated by their presence for another few moments if they were to come back.

The district nurse managed irregular visits, largely to take general observations of pulse and blood pressure and to check for pressure sores. The bed was performing well. At one point her services were required more acutely, to apply a dressing to one of Marie's toes, from which the nail had pulled away. Given the state of the rest of her toenails now, she said she would refer her to Podiatry, but not to hold one's breath waiting for someone to come. Pressure on basic NHS services was dire. Dr Stake continued to visit every two months or so. Brigg had initially anticipated his return, remembering how personable he had been on his first appointment and looking forward to another conversation with him. He was, of course, disappointed. The doctor was professional, but much more perfunctory than on the first visit. By his third visit, he was only in the house for ten minutes. Brigg didn't blame him, nor the nurse; they were understaffed and had miles to drive between appointments, but it was dispiriting and another reason to distance himself from the idea that consolation could be found in the external world. He realised that, whilst Marie remained in a relatively stable state, examinations by health professionals were largely box-ticking exercises, coupled with a gentle surveillance of his own actions. There was little they could do to help Marie. At Stake's fourth visit, Brigg realised that it had now been about six months since the first and he was tempted to ask him about his prognosis that Marie would probably live months, not years. But he did not; after all, what was the point? If he was right, something would happen relatively soon, if he was wrong, then he would have her for longer. Interrogating the doctor about what might have been a rash prediction would achieve nothing.

It was easy to see why the nurse and the doctor were unconcerned. Apart from the fact that she had switched off from the outside world and that her dementia was continuing its slow, inevitable degradation, she was in good health. She was eating and drinking, though sometimes not drinking as much as Brigg would have liked; she was passing urine with no discomfort and had regular bowel movements, albeit managed by Brigg through the administration of the occasional laxative. Her skin was in excellent condition. Her blood pressure tended to be a little on the low side, but perfectly acceptable. The carer visits were usually calm affairs, with few repeats of the early bouts of agitation and distress. Her days passed peacefully. She engaged with the television, gazed out of the window, slept at times, laughed to herself or just lay quietly, seemingly content with where she was. Only once or twice now did she show evidence of painful thoughts, which may have been memories of other times or awareness of her current situation. Who knew? Very occasionally she would appear sad and Brigg would go to try to comfort her, or at least be with her until the sadness passed. But most of the time, she genuinely seemed at peace. As a society, we respond to people with dementia with pity, shrinking from the degradation and confusion it imposes and recoiling with fear at the idea that we all have a chance of being afflicted with this most cruel manifestation of life's randomness. It is that fear, and that response by society, that makes its onset all the more distressing. We have decided that it will result in a lessening of existence, and we react with horror if we are diagnosed. But, as with all conditions that affect the quality of one's engagement in the day-to-day activities of the world, it is the structure of society itself and its attitudes that are the real problem, rather than the individual, unavoidable conditions which are as much a part of 'normality' as any others. We all might get dementia; we all might find ourselves in wheelchairs.

Do not judge the internal quality of life of the person afflicted with such conditions; judge the quality of response of society to them. It is society that excludes them; they do not exclude themselves. Brigg had always agreed with Dr. Stake's idea that all politicians should be made to spend a month in a chair. Only then would they appreciate just how much the way we have organised the world imposed restrictions that need not exist, yet were at the same time accepted by the majority as showing how much wheelchair users were limited and to be pitied.

A cat sleeps for much of the day, but we do not doubt the quality of its internal life, whatever it might be. Yet we consider the internal life of a person with dementia as being partial, no matter how content that person might seem to be. Who has the right, the privileged perspective, to judge another person's quality of life? Who can be the arbiter of when partial becomes complete? Does the concept of 'complete' have any meaning at all? Internal life varies, consciousness varies. No two people will be similarly aware; no two people will inhabit exactly the same world. It is right to say that human beings have a brain which can grant enormous potential, but no single human can claim to be the exemplar of its species in this regard. We have norms of response and understanding, but norms apply to everyone and to no-one. Brigg remembered the lecture he had given that cold November afternoon and the excitement on Holly's face as she had made connections which had extended her conscious awareness and had produced a profound sense of wonder. Perhaps her realisations had made her see things more deeply, or more clearly; certainly, she seemed more elated at the end of the session than at the beginning. He also remembered his rather simplistic, but necessary, philosophical overview. But was Holly any more of a person at the end of the session than at the beginning? Was she any more deserving of respect because she had made connections in her intellectual reasoning that had not been there before? We are conditioned into accepting that intellectual prowess is something to be admired above all else: we have a society which swoons at the minds of the academic elite, constructing a world of ambition that is, and will always be, wholly unattainable by the vast majority. So entrenched are we in this value system that politicians can expand upon attracting the 'brightest and best' to our shores, accompanied by nods of wise, yet mindless, agreement from their fellows. *Best???* Little do they appreciate the content, or the irony, of what they say, or how pernicious the attitude that it represents is to society and our understanding of our lives.

Although it had been a feature of his reflection for as long as he could remember, Brigg was now confronted with the mystery of consciousness on a daily basis. He would gaze at Marie as she lay in bed, sometimes seemingly engaged with the television, sometimes gazing fixedly at a spot in the room, sometimes possessed by a sudden bout of laughter or sadness, or occasionally looking back at him. What was her consciousness? We think of consciousness as fixed, as a thing to be analysed. It is not; it cannot be. Marie was undoubtedly conscious; there was undoubtedly an inner person who was grasping at the world, sometimes with strength, at others apparently only feebly. Was that so different from the rest of us? Where are any of us most of the time? Who can honestly say they inhabit each moment of their day to the same extent of awareness? Gurdjieff used to exhort his students to remember themselves, to become truly aware of their existence in the world. That, for him, was the path for human development. Perhaps. Brigg reflected on how he had been plagued by the quest for consciousness all his life, searching for intensity and finding dissatisfaction and banality in the clutter of necessities that constituted everyday life. Perhaps finding intensity would bring enlightenment and peace, soothing the constant feeling of discontent. But, sometimes, intensity would find him instead, and it did not always bring the peace he wanted. Sometimes, it would only add to the merciless angst that possessed him in the quiet hours of solitude and those moments out of time as he lay awake in the early morning. Were those minutes of fierce intensity any more preferable? Did they define him as a human being? If he had not experienced them, occupying instead the calmer, less stressful consciousness of the everyday, the social, the getting-on-with-the-things-that-have-to-be-done-in-order-to-survive kind of consciousness that formed the bulk of his existence, would he have been a lesser person? Marie was not lesser; she was different. She inhabited forms of consciousness which Brigg had no access to. Were they inferior to his? On what grounds? If it were because they prevented her from maintaining her self in the world, then that was a fair critique, but that also negated his own obsession with intensity: for in his own life it was the intensity that detached him from the easy maintenance of his existence. He could not stop the angst, it would return when he least expected it, as it had done all through his life; but he could challenge it, questioning both its purpose and its usefulness. He had always liked to think that consciousness was the answer; perhaps it was not. He was, after all, merely a reproducing ripple in a vast impersonal stream of genetic chemistry. *Homo sapiens* had no privileged existence; nor did its style of consciousness.

Summer gave way to autumn and the birches turned golden. The midges were finally lessening, the billions of larvae in the limitless dampness of the Highland soil now reaching their final over-wintering phase. Peace returned to both human and cervine populations. Now, Brigg could again walk through the garden unscathed, but with autumn came the shortening of the day and he would soon be restricted to the afternoon should he wish to go outside. Marie had settled into the new rhythm of her confinement and seemed content for him to walk the garden for half an hour whilst it was still light. He would pace around, looking in at her through her window as he completed the short circuit; sometimes, if she were asleep, going down to the lochside for a little while to gaze over the water and lose himself in the hills. Those moments became precious; they were important exercise but also deeply refreshing.

There was no wind and a silver light played on the still waters of the loch. The tide was in. The tips of the wrack could be seen floating against the surface of the water lapping against the rough shore, momentarily calm before resuming the endless cycle of ebb and flow. The sides of Cruachan were sharp in the clear air, but the summits of the horseshoe hid themselves in a thin veil of cloud that shrouded the land in a November requiem for the passing year. He felt the presence of an invisible tie binding him to the house and Marie in the bed, but he was relaxed, secure in his proximity and the knowledge that, even if she awoke from her gentle sleep, she would not fret that he was not in the room. The television provided the reassurance she needed. He always came back.

Such beauty. Some would agree, some would recoil from the empty starkness of the landscape. None of that mattered;

this was his beauty: the culmination of senses, emotion and life history that made his unique being revel in the moment of its existence in the place. Despite all that was Marie, all that he was powerless to affect, he was fortunate. He had this moment. There would be another moment when all his time as John Brigg would cease, but, as Dawkins so beautifully expressed, that made him lucky; he would die because he was lucky to be alive. Countless billions of potential humans didn't even have the opportunity to have the history that gave them beauty. Somehow, he was here, now, experiencing. Alive.

Was it real? Were the idealists right all along that this world we experience is no more than a product of an ineffable consciousness that existed before there was ever an awareness to imagine a world that could bestow such delight? A consciousness that rippled and flowed in a space and time of its own making, teasing itself with whirlpools and eddies of fleeting individuality before absorbing them into the substrate of which they had always been? Or, as he had outlined to the group that similar November day so many years ago now, should we simply accept the evidence of our daily existence and trust the intuitive veracity of the materialist assertions that what we think we see is what is really there? There could be no conclusive refutation from the idealists, for although, as they correctly asserted, our perceptual access to our world lies in our minds, their conclusion that this demonstrates that the world is solely mental is fallacious. It is an example of 'affirming the consequent'. But, likewise, materialists could have no ultimate proof of their constructed world. So much is taken for granted in the materialist perspective, and the disturbing implications of the questions being raised as physicists immerse themselves gleefully in the mind-bending world of quantum strangeness, are conveniently ignored. Materialism as a philosophy inhabits finite, time-limited universes, accepting that space, time, matter and all that can be known, came into existence at the Big Bangs that created them, or, perhaps, just the single one that we seem to have definite knowledge of. But there is no more certain proof for that than there is for idealism, save for our supposedly shared experience.

The tide had sent the geese inland to try their luck on the moorland grass and the small amount of cultivated land around the loch and coastal shores. But there was a small, loosely cohesive group of waders picking their way through the small stones by the water's edge, eagerly harvesting the plentiful gammarids, slaters and other small creatures that were just beyond the level of this high tide. He watched in delight as two industrious ringed plovers came within two metres of him, pecking incessantly at prey too small or too fleeting for his eyes to see. Every now and then, one would stop, sit back on its short orange legs and puff out its little black and white streaked chest with all the confidence of a creature secure in its position in the world. It would seem to glance at Brigg's stationary form from behind its highwayman's mask, then resume its scavenging without a moment of concern. Plover time was too short to worry about the lumbering creatures that sometimes strayed into the vicinity of the lochside.

Plover time. Plover consciousness? Who knew? But whatever it was like to be a plover, he was sure that they did not bother themselves with the impenetrable tangle of intellectual analysis that beset the human condition. Not for them was the concern for materialism or idealism, or the dualist hedging of the bets so beloved by religions and philosophers like Chalmers, who had now seemingly taken abstruseness to its ultimate, identifying a further 'meta-problem', which would try to explore what the experience of having the 'hard problem' was actually like. Sometimes Brigg envied the creatures that got on with life rather than being plagued by it, as he so often had been.

He could not reconcile himself with idealism, with the idea that all was a mental construction, no matter how much he could not refute it. Looking back on his life, he had no evidence that his consciousness could exist without his body, even if, as he well knew, association does not prove anything. But, surely, the mistake lay in thinking of consciousness as a thing, a given. It was not. When he was born, he was not conscious at all; it would take about two years before self-reflection would start to appear. It would change and develop as he grew into adulthood, but it was not something that had been achieved; it was still coming, still developing, fluctuating, at times intense, at others hardly there. It had developed as his brain had developed. Was that association not enough to deduce cause and effect? If he had stayed as an infant, with the rudimentary complexity of his brain at that age, he would never have developed the mature self-awareness of adult consciousness. It needed another fifteen years of development, change, reshaping, rejection and re-wiring of neurons during puberty before something approaching that capacity for consciousness consolidated itself in his 'human' being. As it did so, it refined the thread of narrative that he called himself, sometimes starkly, achingly intense, often simply flickering and regularly switching off as his body slept. He took it for granted each night that it would return, but perhaps one day it would not and he knew that even if it did, it could still be moulded by anaesthesia or degraded into a semi-rational state by the brain-eating march of dementia.

Was it enough to deduce cause and effect? His rational, objective mind thought so, but in the solitary depths of his awareness, he knew that the argument was just another facet of his constructed existence. It was logical, well-supported by evidence and difficult to refute, but none of that meant it was true, whatever that might mean. The curse of the Western world is that its philosophy and over two thousand years of Judeo-Christianity straight-jackets the awareness of its people with an ideal of truth. It is so difficult to relinquish the idea, even whilst one knows that it is an impossible aspiration. No epistemology that we have ever devised can deliver truth. But we are incapable of turning away from the quest, and there lies the source of our angst. We are still like children; we still expect that someone will eventually take us on one side in this classroom of life and tell us that we have chosen correctly, that we are 'right'. But the teacher has gone, our parents know no more than we do, the law is a construct and our ethics and values are merely memes. We are on our own. We have to take the responsibility. He knew the questions would plague him until the moment of his death and, for all their unattainability, they were what made him who he was.

Plato suggested that there was a real world of ideals, of which this world was merely a shadow; dualists continue this narrative with their conceptions of separate minds and bodies and their visions of eternity and heaven; idealists consider that all is consciousness and that our experience of the world is just a product of that consciousness, manifesting itself through our individual minds; materialists consider that what you see is what you get: matter is real, it is subject to inexorable processes and that whatever you are, you are a product of them. None of the perspectives can claim truth, and Brigg knew that the critical mind has to remain sceptical of them all. Although there has always been much cross-fertilisation between them and even Hume acknowledged that our perceptions were a product of our minds, it seemed to Brigg that there was now a distinct tendency to separate into camps. He could not follow that trend, for all perspectives offered meaning to him at some level.

Despite his scientific training, in his youth he had harboured ideas of hidden forces and esoteric knowledge that underpinned the world, which someday he would gain access to and thus understand the true meaning of everything. In those days, he would have recoiled from the hard materialist reasoning of Dennett and Dawkins and their acceptance of a finite world with no meaning other than that which its inhabitants could generate for themselves. But why should that be repelling? With age, a realisation had come to him that he had been forever trying to reject the only experience he ever truly had: his existence in a concrete world where he lived, loved, ate, defaecated, felt pain, joy, excitement and enervation. Why should he reject what was blindingly obvious, in search of an alternative that never came? Dennett's idea of consciousness as a user-illusion was not threatening; in fact, it pulled together many strands of logical thinking. Simply because he labelled it an illusion did not change the experience of having it; that was not what he meant. Yes, there is consciousness, but don't look for it as something other than a feature of what is going on naturally within our bodies. It is not a separate thing to be isolated. Now, Brigg could see that

Dennett's thinking was coherent and cogent. Over hundreds of millions of years of evolution, neural processes had laid down network upon network of patterns of increasing complexity. Layer upon layer existed in the brain, supplemented by behavioural and cultural memes which spread through populations and passed from generation to generation through mimicry and learning. Dennett claimed that to think that these processes somehow generated a new entity called consciousness was wrong: what consciousness consisted of was a kind of user interface with them, analogous to the files, folders and windows of a laptop screen. There are no files or folders inside the computer; the icons simply build an illusion so that you can use it. In a similar way, Dennett argued, consciousness was a user-illusion generated by the brain, generating out of the ancient neural patterns evolved over millennia illusions of colour, warmth, love and all the extraordinary experience of living. If one stopped thinking of consciousness as being something separate to be examined *per se*, it solved the difficulties of other materialist explanations, which very swiftly arrived at Chalmer's hard problem and often veered off towards some form of dualism. In many ways, Brigg found it a liberating idea: rather than asking him to reject the whole of his life's experience, it validated it and placed him back in the heart of the story of evolving life on this planet. Everywhere he looked, he could see evidence that consciousness was an emergent facility, and surely the place to look for a mechanism had to be within the development of complex neural activity and the processing of cultural behavioural practices that had accrued over millennia. What other database do we have? Dennett had merely been consistent. No matter how much we would like to think otherwise, evolution was not pulled from above, it drove from below. It did not have purpose; creatures did not strive to achieve new body forms. That Dawkins' theory of the selfish gene left church leaders and much of the population aghast, said more about the extent to which we have all been brainwashed into thinking that we somehow occupy a special place in the world. The only special place we occupy is the potential scourge we present to the rest of the planet, through our burgeoning population and our inability to use wisely the consciousness that our brains produce.

Coherent, yes; satisfying, possibly. It depended on his state of mind. As a theory, it had internal consistency and it made strong logical sense. It seemed to mop up other theories that he had been attracted to, such as Julian Jaynes' intriguing idea of self-consciousness emerging out of an initial 'bicameralism' in the brain. But he was always left with the paradox of the illusion itself. If it were only an illusion, where did that leave the products of the illusion's activity? Dennett's idea had emerged from the workings of his illusion; his conclusions were tested in consciousness, not in the layer upon layer of responses programmed through aeons of neural development and cultural experience that he claimed made up the raw material of cognition. Yet this paradox could also explain why our searching could never give us truth; truth was not a part of the initial conditions of the programming. Life did not need truth; it needed success.

So, if it was coherent and persuasive, why couldn't he fully commit to it? As Brigg watched the birds move on, he heard the lonely three-note piping of a redshank as it flew over the loch. His heart leaped. It had been one of the first wild bird calls that he had become familiar with and it took him back fifty years to his student days, when he had spent time in the wide salt marshes of Langstone and Chichester harbours. He loved the call; it was a mournful sound, yet it filled him with joy. It never ceased to engender an intense awareness of his own individuality in the landscape. How could this individuality be an illusion? It was in this individuality that he found the deepest solace and happiness. There was no surrendering of himself to the transcendence of idealism; it had always been the intense realisation of his existence in and alongside the world that was the seat of that happiness. It gave him unity, but it was a unity in which he was both one and many: an active realisation, not a passive process. As far back as he could remember, at moments like these he had felt that unity with other living things, and with the land, the rocks, the mountains and the sea. His individuality was hard and detached, yet wholly connected. If there was anywhere he needed to explore to find answers, it was that individuality. Dennett would say the awareness was all part of the user-illusion; idealists would also dismiss it as illusory, as nothing more than a localised excitation in the underlying randomness of pure mind. He could commit to neither as the piping faded away and the water gleamed against the farther shore.

He had not been complete in his summary to the students that afternoon. As he had intimated to Ben at the end of the session, he did not consider all three perspectives to be of equal merit. Dualism he found absurd. It was a logical contradiction; surely what was, was. The implication of dualism that there could exist parallel worlds, one of which ultimately could be of no consequence, was an affront to his reasoning. The world, mind, consciousness, physicality, was a whole, it had to be. However, more important than the irritation he felt with dualism, there was another way of approaching consciousness that he had not mentioned. Spurned by all other perspectives as illogical or even as a philosophy of madness, solipsism had plagued him all his adult life, even before he knew of the name, and nothing could eradicate its relentless logic. Those bouts of intense awareness of his own individuality had begun in his teens. As he had become aware of his own isolation in the world, he had begun to juxtapose it against the other billions upon billions of consciousnesses that existed or must have existed. It had caused him both wonder and fear as he had viewed the rest of existence from the unique awareness that was himself. Since then, nothing, not idealist, materialist, dualist or any other perspective, had explained satisfactorily to him how that could be. It simply did not make sense. Who was he? When he contemplated the world, everything – *everything* – was 'other'. There was only him in a third-person world of everything else. Would it exist if he were not there? Why was there a consciousness in the world that was conscious as him? It did not need to exist, yet it did, and all that he could or would ever know about the world was a product of it. Yes, it might be a philosophy of madness, but simply calling it that did not argue it away. Rather than madness, it was a philosophy of logical consistency, for all his reasoning only took place inside his mind. It occurred nowhere else. He battled against its absurdity daily, and it would recede at times, but it never wholly went away.

Perhaps the only argument he could think of that seemed to refute it, lay in challenging the fundamental premise on which it was built. Solipsism implied, much as did Descartes, that the only thing knowable is one's consciousness. But surely that was fallacious. Brigg could not know himself independently of his relation to something outside himself. His conception of himself, as a 'me' in the world, was meaningless unless it was in relation to something else. Without that relation, there was no self-awareness, for self only had meaning in relation to not-self. If all that existed were inside himself, he would only be able to find reality by emptying his consciousness of the clutter of an imagined outside world that he had created. But in order to do this, he would have to negate a key element of the nature of consciousness itself: that of consciousness-in-relation. Consciousness-not-in-relation, suggested by pure solipsism, was a contradiction. Consciousness must have an object.

So many contradictions, so many doubts, so many questions. Like Goethe's Faust, he looked back on his life and wondered if he was any wiser than when he had started out. The adolescent certainty of answers had receded long ago and now he was content, at least most of the time, with acceptance. Dennett and Dawkins were a consolation in such a world-view and they helped him understand the person Marie had become. They helped him detach from the tyranny of searching for meaning and the sense that she was somehow less than she had been. There was no less and no more; she was what she was. We were so used to conceptualising *things*, that our language and communication obscured the fact that existence is no more than a moment of becoming. No more, perhaps, but in that moment there was everything. The past no longer exists, the future has yet to be generated. All is now, and in that ever-evolving moment, he found a peace. It was a peace that came from knowing that existing was sufficient in itself; it was a triumph of improbability and it did not need goals or promises of better things to come. It had to be sufficient, for he knew that there was nothing else for him, nor could there be. In a twist of irony, life was giving him his broadest vision as his boundaries were ostensibly the narrowest they had ever been. If joy were not to be found within that moment of existence, with no justification other than it was there, it would not be found at all.

Brigg knew he had to return; he had already been away longer than usual. He had been lost in his reverie. He was not concerned, but he knew she would be awake by now and, besides, the carers would be returning shortly for their afternoon visit. The high water was already starting to recede, granting the birds a wider area of exposed shoreline for their scavenging. He turned away, up the grass to the road and then over to the house. The light was starting to fade, and at this time of the year darkness would soon fall. He needed to put a light on in Marie's room and check the heating for the evening. He shut the front door firmly, so she would hear he was in the house again, slipped off his outdoor shoes, changing into an old, comfortable pair that he kept for inside use. He could hear the television in Marie's room. He went in.

She was lying calmly, her head resting comfortably on the pillow and watching an antiques programme. She did not move as he entered. He flicked on a lamp on the table by her bed and checked that her drinks beaker was full. He stood for a few moments resting his hands on the padded metal side of the bed, watching the programme with her. She did not turn to him or otherwise give any indication that she knew he had come in. Perhaps, in her mind now, he was always there, visible or not visible. He was a feature, a security, a constant in her tiny outer world of the room, the television and the view through the window. But who knew where her inner world took her now, or how big it was? Wherever she was, she looked content.

"The carers will be back soon," he said; "and then I'll think about some tea."

She did not respond. Brigg left the room and returned a minute later holding a bottle of beer. He held it up between Marie and the television so she could see it.

"I fancy a beer," he said. "Would you like some?"

Marie's focus switched slowly from the television to the bottle he was holding in front of her. She stared at it for a few moments, as though she was processing its nature. Then, finally, she turned her head towards him. A broad grin spread across her face, filling Brigg's heart.

"Lovely!" she exclaimed.

Printed in Great Britain
by Amazon